Brooke bit her l[...] she was taking, [...] not to back down. He may not see her as a wife, but she wanted, at least, some kind of a relationship with him that didn't make them strangers. "You have me."

Jameson set the flowers aside, then pulled Brooke into his embrace. "Is this what you had in mind?" he whispered into her ear.

Brooke briefly shut her eyes, pressed her cheek against his chest and held him close. "Yes." She drew away and looked up at him. She opened her mouth to say more, but he smothered her words with a kiss.

Unlike the kiss at the ceremony, she knew this one was meant only for her, and that made it sweeter than she could have imagined. For a moment it made her thoughts spin, and she imagined him wanting her as much as she wanted him. She wrapped her arms around his neck and deepened the kiss. Jameson moaned with satisfaction. His hand dipped to her blouse. "Are you wearing anything from your trousseau underneath this?"

"No, but I can—"

"We'll save them for another time," he said, removing her blouse.

Books by Dara Girard

Harlequin Kimani Romance

Sparks
The Glass Slipper Project
Taming Mariella
Power Play
A Gentleman's Offer
Body Chemistry
Round the Clock
Words of Seduction
Pages of Passion
Beneath the Covers
All I Want Is You
Secret Paradise
A Reluctant Hero
Perfect Match
Snowed in with the Doctor
Engaging Brooke

Harlequin Kimani Arabesque

Table For Two
Gaining Interest
Carefree
Illusive Flame

DARA GIRARD

fell in love with storytelling at an early age. Her romance writing career happened by chance when she discovered the power of a happy ending. She is an award-winning author whose novels are known for their sense of humor, interesting plot twists and witty dialogue. When she's not writing, she enjoys spring mornings and autumn afternoons, French pastries, dancing to the latest hits and long drives.

Dara loves to hear from her readers. You can reach her at contactdara@daragirard.com or P.O. Box 10345, Silver Spring, MD 20914.

Dara Girard

Engaging
BROOKE

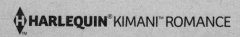
HARLEQUIN® KIMANI™ ROMANCE

Recycling programs
for this product may
not exist in your area.

ISBN-13: 978-0-373-86353-2

ENGAGING BROOKE

Printed in U.S.A.

Dear Reader,

Okay, I'll be honest. I was the last person who thought she'd ever write about a cowboy hero. I mean, what did a kid of immigrants know about something so quintessentially American? But when my editor offered me the opportunity to be part of The Browards of Montana series, I was up for the challenge.

Researching about ranch life and talking to friends who have horses and farm animals (thank you!) really made me appreciate those who are part of a long-standing history. And I saw a lot of commonality with the immigrant journey—grit, cunning, and love of land and family.

Which brings me to Jameson Broward. A man who encompasses that and more. He's been burned by love and is unwilling to share his heart again…but you know what that means. He's going to fall hard.

My first cowboy hero…I'm as surprised as you are.

Enjoy,

Dara Girard

Chapter 1

They were under attack. That was the only way Jameson Broward could describe it. The town as they knew it was being seized by an unknown buyer. Longtime residents were being wooed by the charm of easy money instead of realizing the magnitude of the consequences of selling their land to outsiders who may not have the town's best interest in mind. Jameson looked around at his family as they sat in the BWB Great Room. The Great Room, which was the centerpiece in the elegant main house of the Broward Webb Broward Heritage Ranch, always served as the perfect place to discuss business—both personal and professional.

Grandpa Charles, the family patriarch, pounded the side of his chair with his fist. "I want to know what's going on. I want to know where we're headed before we get there. Who is doing this?" he said, asking the question they all wanted to know the answer to. Why had their beloved town of Granger, Montana, suddenly been thrust into the spotlight by an unnamed investor—or several investors for that matter, they weren't sure how many interested people there were.

That's what worried Jameson the most. The lack of transparency. Unfortunately, however, one particular land sale had been made clear, brutally so, and had struck him and his entire family in the heart.

"What can we do about Wes?" his mother, Gwendolyn Broward asked. She sat across from him, poised and graceful like the professional horsewoman she was. She was worried, very much so, but kept her voice and features calm. She was an attractive woman whose youthful looks belied her age of fifty-six.

"Nothing. The land is gone," his father, Steven, said as he stroked his graying beard. Jameson could hear the hurt and dismay in his voice. His father, Charles, along with his three brothers had been responsible for developing their land into a lucrative ranching business. Millions of dollars, and years of blood and sweat, had gone into creating the family business they expected to keep.

Betrayal. He'd experienced it before, but he hadn't expected it from his own flesh and blood. Jameson knew that just like him, his father felt hurt by what his younger son, Wes, had done. Without telling anyone, he'd sold his land to Samara Lionne, a Hollywood actress no less. Yes, Jameson's brother was the reason for the family get-together. Not the buying up of the town, not even the mystery of the buyers, but the fact that a member of their own family had completed a substantial transaction without telling them.

Although, technically the land he sold was not part of their family land, it was still Granger land, and they all felt it shouldn't have been sold to an outsider. They'd known Wes had been entertaining buyers, but they'd never thought he'd go through with a sale without at least warning them or giving them an option to buy it themselves. But, either in an act of cowardice or just pure luck, Wes hadn't stuck around to deal with the ramifications of his actions. He was off traveling in Europe with his fiancée, Lydia. Jameson didn't like to think too cruelly of his brother, but he always knew that Wes had never loved the land the way Jameson and the rest of the family did. The land was Jameson's life. His heart. It was the one thing that never betrayed him. It never let him down. The ranch and the town of Granger were all he had and he would fight to the death to maintain it for generations to come.

And, just like the rest of the family, Jameson had a feeling something shady was going on. They needed to find out what. Both his father and grandfather had been unable to get straight answers from people in town or their trusted friends. Unfortunately, over time, many of the old-timers of Granger had either retired and moved away or had died or, as was the case with most of the current residents, their children were more like Wes and were looking for ways to make money off the land.

Gwendolyn shook her head, casting a quick glance at Jameson as if she expected him to say something. He remained silent. "Why didn't he just come to us? We would have bought it from him."

"I never thought I'd live to see the day one of us would *sell* land instead of buy it," Grandpa Charles said, for a moment looking older than his eighty-four years. His blue eyes tired, he also sent Jameson a look as if hoping he could add something, but Jameson looked away. Charles had grown up on the land that his father, Silas Broward, had claimed as a homestead in the 1930s. While the Depression's strong grip decimated lives in the big cities, Silas had built up the ranch one horse at a time, raising four sons with his wife, Olivia. Charles and his brother, Stanley, grew the Broward Ranch into a highly successful cattle breeding operation. Stanley also raised four sons who had prospered and owned ranches in another part of Montana.

Jameson felt that ranching wasn't just a family tradition. It was a calling. He knew that both his father and grandfather wanted him to speak at this gathering, but he had nothing to say. Nothing that could be said to his family. He was seething but kept his face a neutral mask. His brother had a right to do what he wanted with his land. Because it wasn't part of the BWB Ranch, it wouldn't affect their bottom line, but it was the recklessness that bothered him. And the fact that Wes always did exactly what he wanted as long as it made him happy. It didn't bother Wes that outsiders were sweeping into Granger like vultures to taint the pristine land with their foolhardy dreams of ranch or farm work, most of which they had seen romanticized on TV and in the movies. He looked at his younger sister, Laney, who was unusually quiet.

"Is there any way to talk to this woman?" Gwendolyn asked.

Steven sighed. "Damn it, I told you he did it too quickly for us to do anything."

"Change is on its way," Grandpa Charles said. "But sometimes it worries me. This ranch was built up one horse at a time, but others see a quick buck and don't care about the people or this place. They don't care that there are people who depend on us. Granger has been a major employer for cowboys and ranch hands who want to work the land."

"Dad, things will work out," Steven said to his father. He quickly looked at Jameson as if he wanted him to speak up. Jameson folded his arms instead. "Besides, it was Wes's land. It was not officially a part of our family heritage. So, he had the right and freedom to sell it to whomever he wanted and for whatever amount he wanted. I just wish he had given us a chance."

Excuses. All Jameson heard his father say were excuses. Excuses for Wes. Excuses to explain away how his younger son's actions had hurt them.

"Jameson," Steven finally said, clearly the only one brave enough to involve him in the conversation. They all had been sending glances to him, as if he were a volcano they expected to erupt. But he was too controlled for that. Yes, he was furious. He was enraged by a feeling of helplessness he couldn't contain, but exposing how he felt wouldn't be something he'd let them see again. They'd seen it once before, more than ten years ago when a woman had ripped his heart apart.

At twenty-two, Meredith Palmer, the woman he'd planned to spend the rest of his life with, had ended their relationship. She'd been his first love. She was his high school sweetheart and after they'd graduated, they'd maintained a long-distance romance while he'd studied agribusiness at Montana State University in Bozeman and she'd attended a college back East. He'd imagined them growing old together and making his family's business even more successful than his father had. But with one phone call a few weeks before his graduation from college, she'd dashed his hopes.

"I've met someone else," she'd said over the phone, as if she was reciting a weather report. Her words had been cool, practiced. What she had to say was stated without a single sign of emotion, while every word pierced his heart.

"What do you mean?"

"I can't marry you."

Jameson thought of all the people who expected them to get married. Damn, he'd expected it. He'd had his whole life planned and at that moment it was coming apart at the seams. He knew he couldn't win her back, and frankly, he didn't want to. Years before he'd even looked at another woman.

He'd thought Priscilla Clark would make a perfect rancher's wife. But he soon learned he'd been wrong. He should have known it wouldn't work from the beginning. For one, she'd kept calling him "James," which he hated. But he'd forgiven her all her faults, primarily because she was very pretty, beautiful in fact, and stroked his ego. He'd introduced her to his family and he didn't care that the reception had been cool. His parents had been enthusiastic about Meredith and he'd seen how that had turned out. He'd gotten some subtle warnings from his Grandpa Charles, who'd said, "Be careful. A hungry man can find anything appetizing." His father had been more to the point: "Any woman who can't get your name right is after something else." But, at that time, he didn't care because Priscilla listened to him, unlike Meredith. She didn't say anything disparaging about ranching and she told him how wonderful he was, which was all he needed to hear. Then one day he had traveled to Smithville, one of Granger's neighboring towns, and overheard Priscilla talking to a friend in the grocery store.

"Oh, my God!" Priscilla said in a stage whisper. "You should see his parents' place."

"Well, I heard the Browards are loaded," her friend said.

"Loaded is too humble a term. When I marry James I'm going to be rolling in money."

"He's asked you to marry him?"

"He hasn't yet. But he will and I'm going to get him to build me a house as big as his parents'. No, even bigger. I have really hit the jackpot with this one. I usually don't like going after men that other women have dumped, but this is one leftover I'm ready to reheat. I won't have to use my degree because I'm going to be well taken care of. Mom was right when she told me to set my eyes on him. Men wallowing in heartbreak are so easy to use. And I'll make him grateful to have me. I know his brother, Wes, would be a lot more fun, but he's not ready to settle down like James."

That's when he'd finally realized that she only saw dollar signs when she looked at him. He'd never be seen as someone's leftovers. He never told Priscilla why he broke it off, and the devastation on her face had almost made him smile. At that moment he vowed that women weren't for him. Since then, he'd thought he could always trust his land and his family at least, but now Wes had taught him that he couldn't even trust that.

"Jameson," Steven repeated. "Don't you have anything to say?"

"No."

"Did you know what Wes was up to?"

Jameson lowered his gaze and brushed imaginary lint from his sleeve. "I never know what he's up to."

Without his input the conversation floundered, as he hoped it would. He felt as if a fire was burning inside him, and talking about what Wes had done only added gasoline. Jameson needed to get away, to think of what his next step should be. The town was under threat and it would take a cool head to strategize how to handle the situation.

He lifted his gaze and sounded bored. "Are we done?"

His father nodded. Jameson stood and went out back. He needed to be outdoors. He stood in the doorway that led to the backyard and smelled the May morning air. How could someone love anything less than all this? Jameson looked out on the acres of land in front of him.

The land stretched on for miles and miles and looked like a landscape painting. He loved the emerald-green grass against the backdrop of the rugged mountain range in the distance, dotted with the earthy, smooth, brown bodies of his cattle. Low-hanging trees provided a framework through which to see the land; to him it was more than beautiful. It was his life. He was determined. He wouldn't let his grandfather or father down. He'd maintain BWB. He couldn't—no, wouldn't—let their heritage end with him.

"Don't be too angry with Wes," his mom, Gwendolyn, said as she came up behind him.

Jameson kept his gaze on the horizon, watching the rolling prairie grass undulate in the breeze. He loved his mother but knew she didn't understand his deep connection to the ranch and to the land. He wasn't as fun-loving as Wes or an accomplished horseman like his sister, Laney. At times he felt like a throwback to another time. A time when being a man who valued his land and family mattered. "It was his land to do with as he wanted," Jameson said, wishing he could feel as casual and nonchalant as he sounded. "He knew what he was doing and didn't have to tell us about it."

"I don't think he thought of it that way. Times are changing and—"

Jameson spun around to her. "Not that much. Have times changed so much that you don't think about one's responsibilities or family loyalties?"

Gwendolyn lightly touched his cheek, the same soothing touch she'd give a lame horse. Although the gesture annoyed him, it also calmed him as she knew it would. "You're doing the best you can."

And what if it's not enough? What if I lose everything? He wanted to say this, but instead he turned away, keeping his fears to himself, just as he did everything else. "Do you think Grandpa Charles deserves to see the day when all he's struggled to build is destroyed because of greed? Well, I won't let that happen."

"When are you going to start a family of your own?"

Jameson shook his head, his voice low. "I don't have time for that now."

"You have to make time."

"I went on a date, didn't I?"

"That was for charity," his mother said, referring to the recent bachelor charity auction that was an annual town event. "Besides, I know you hate being a part of that every year."

Jameson shrugged without concern. His mother was right. "It was still a date," he said, leaving no room for argument. The Browards were known for their charity work, and it was one of the few events he had been unable to avoid.

He heard her soft sigh before his mother turned and went back inside.

Jameson stepped out on the deck. He had the blood of a rancher running through his veins. His family had put the small town of Granger, Montana, on the map. He remembered being five years old and feeling the calloused hands of his grandpa as he led him around the ranch. From an early age he loved the smell of the cattle, horses, chickens and pigs. By three, even before he could read, he could pick out a heifer from a cow. As he got older, he'd loved learning to rope a calf and ride a horse, drinking fresh milk and smelling Montana grass, which, to him, was the best in the world. At seven he had been given his own flock of chickens and several pigs to care for and a dog he called Buddy. He had respect for all the animals. He could read them better than he could any person. Maybe that's why he felt so comfortable on the ranch. Animals would not betray him. They would not connive or deceive. He decided to make sure that Wes's action, along with others, didn't do the damage to Granger he feared, which was putting power into the hands of a group of people who didn't care about the town.

Granger was becoming unrecognizable to him, with outsiders, mostly from the city, thinking themselves ranchers. His parents had money flowing into their lodge-style estate, which they had successfully turned into a business. Gwendolyn had been the one to first make the suggestion of turning the main house into a money-making venture. At first, his father had objected, but once he saw it in operation, he was on board.

They had turned only half of the main house on the BWB Ranch into a rental lodge and had maintained the upper floors as their private family residence. And business was booming. They had reservations scheduled over the next two years. Under Gwendolyn's expert guidance, they had developed several vacation packages including a bed-and-breakfast experience, a tour of the range and the chance to spend a week with the ranch hands. Their most famous package allowed guests to "rough it" for three days—living in tents, milking cows, and either fishing or hunting for their food and cooking whatever they caught on an open fire.

Jameson respected people who understood the hard work that came with cattle ranching and horse breeding, but people with more money than sense bothered him. He knew his grandfather and parents were worried and they had every right to be. A private buyer could change what Granger was all about, and he wouldn't let that happen. He vowed he'd prove himself and make the Broward name shine even brighter than it did now.

His cell phone rang. "Hello?"

"We just lost one," his foreman said.

Jameson lowered his head and swore. He knew he couldn't say too much for fear of being overheard by the house staff. No one in his family knew what he'd been up to and if they did, he'd never hear the end of it. He'd taken a risk and lost, but it wouldn't affect anyone but him. "How's the other one?"

"Touch and go."

"Thanks. I'll be over there soon." Jameson hung up. It seemed to be a day full of pain, but he was used to it. He knew how to handle himself now. He'd stay focused on work and his family because he had no room in his life for more than that. He'd given his heart away once, to Meredith, and had had it broken. The second time, with Priscilla, he'd let his male organ rule and that had gotten him in trouble, too. He knew that his intellect was the only thing that would save him. And help him save what mattered to him. He made a promise to himself that he'd never love another person as much as he loved his land and animals. And he kept his promises.

Gwendolyn returned to the main living room, where her husband sat, sipping on a cup of coffee.

"Well," Steven said patting the seat beside him. "Were you able to talk to him? Does he have any idea of what we can do to stop us from losing more of Granger?"

Gwendolyn sat down next to her husband of thirty-four years and sighed. He usually was able to make her feel better, but not this time. Jameson really had them both worried. "No, he's keeping to himself as usual. He always handles stress by withdrawing. He won't talk about Wes selling the land or anything else."

"He wasn't always like that."

Gwendolyn knew she didn't need to reply. They both were aware the painful breakup with Meredith had changed Jameson. He'd been a little more carefree, not so solitary, when he was younger. They both missed that son who could laugh during a Montana rainstorm and talked about the future with optimism.

"No man should let a woman have that much of an effect on him," Steven said with feeling.

"It wasn't just Meredith—it was that other woman, too. What was her name?"

"Who cares what her name was? The problem is there's been no other woman since then to compare her to. He won't date. He won't even consider a dating service both online or off. I don't know what we're going to do with that boy."

"He's not ready."

Steven shook his head. "I just don't want him thinking that this place is all that life is about. I want him to have a family of his own. And so does Dad. Besides, there are plenty of other women for him to choose from. He's just too stubborn to notice."

Gwendolyn nodded. "He's stubborn and proud. That won't be an easy mix for a woman to take on. Sometimes I fear that there's no woman who will be able to break through his wall."

Chapter 2

The stares and whispers didn't surprise her. Brooke Palmer walked onto the Broward Ranch with her head held high and her insides trembling. In the distance she saw herds of cows grazing and men on horses. Although other ranches now used dirt bikes and four-wheelers, the Browards still used horses to move cattle through the rough and steep terrain. But no one was paying attention to that; everyone was staring at her. She was the anomaly. A Palmer had not been on Broward land in the past ten years and it was all her sister's fault. Meredith had been a fool to let Jameson go and damage the tie the Browards and Palmers had. Back then, if Brooke had been older than fifteen, she would have asked Jameson to marry her instead.

She'd dreamed of showing up in a white wedding

dress at the church and telling Jameson to marry her. She understood him in a way she felt no one else did. At times, he seemed to stand in the shadow of his father, whose radical ways of breeding high-end cattle and heritage farm animals had made them incredibly wealthy. His father also had secured an advantageous marriage into the Webb family, who'd made their fortune breeding rare stallions and quadrupled the profits of the ranch. Jameson wasn't as charming as his younger brother, Wes, but she thought he was better looking. His intense ways could be off-putting, but she knew how much he loved the land and, from her point of view, he was all a man should be.

Unfortunately, Brooke knew that Jameson saw her as a child. He'd never looked at her the way he'd looked at her sister and other women. She was just a little girl to him. He was a man planning his future. She'd even thought of buying him at the recent cowboy charity auction, but she hadn't been bold enough, considering the history between their families. But now she had a reason to meet with him. She knew he wasn't a man who liked to date, but she wondered what he thought about marriage.

Brooke took a deep breath then raised her hand to knock on the door just as it swung open. Laney took a step back in surprise. Jameson's younger sister was as beautiful in person as she was in all the pictures taken of her. Even more striking actually.

"Hi, Laney," Brooke said when the other woman just stared.

Laney shook her head, as if coming out of a stupor.

"Hi." She opened the door wider. "Sorry, I'm just surprised to see you."

"Congratulations on your medals. It must be hard getting back to the ordinary life and routine of Granger."

"No, it's a relief."

When she didn't expand, Brooke searched her mind for something else to say. "You look great."

"Thanks."

Brooke shifted, feeling awkward. Laney obviously didn't want to talk. She was usually more bubbly, but she seemed quiet and reserved. Perhaps she resented her for being the sister of a woman who'd broken her brother's heart. "I don't want to keep you. You were getting ready to go somewhere. I just want to see Jameson."

Laney gestured for her to come inside, clearly eager to leave. "Oh, he's in the back of the house, gazing at his mistress."

Brooke felt her heart race. "Mistress?"

"You know," she called over her shoulder as she stepped outside. "The ranch."

"Right," Brooke said, feeling her pulse return to normal. "Thanks," she said, but Laney was already out of hearing range. Even though Jameson had his own house on the property, people knew he spent most of his time at the main house. Brooke closed the door then walked through the hallway off to the side and saw Mr. and Mrs. Broward sitting in the Great Room. They stared at her, stunned.

"Hello," she said, wanting to break the silence. She absently pointed to a vague space down the hall. "Laney told me Jameson was down here."

"How have you been?" Steven said. "We were sorry to hear about your father."

"Well, thank you."

Gwendolyn stood up. "Where are my manners? It's lovely to see you. Would you like something to drink or—?"

"No," Brooke said, relieved that their welcome had been a bit more cordial than Laney's. That gave her hope that the favor she needed from Jameson might get a good response. "I just need to ask Jameson something."

"Well, if you need anything let us know."

"I will." Brooke headed to the back of the house and saw Jameson standing just outside the doorway. As he stood staring at the horizon, she took a moment to stare at him. She looked at him through the eyes of an artist. If she were to paint him, she'd depict him as a landscape with shoulders as wide as the Montana sky, skin smooth as the sharp edge of a canyon and height as tall as a mountain. He was lean but muscular, with the intensity of a raging river. Her heart began racing, even though she'd told it to behave. Jameson had always had that kind of effect on her.

Brooke opened the door and cleared her throat to let him know she was there and not startle him.

Jameson didn't turn and he didn't seem startled; it was as if he already knew she was there. "Yes? What do you want?" he said, his voice a low, deep rumble.

Brooke swallowed. If he could affect her like this with his back to her, how would she fare when he faced her? She had to find out.

"I want to talk to you," she said, her voice higher than she wanted, but steady.

She saw his shoulders stiffen. It was just a flash and if she hadn't known him so well, she wouldn't have seen it. He turned, in a slow, deliberate manner that only increased the anticipation of seeing his face again. His cowboy hat kept his face in shadow, so she couldn't clearly read his expression. Brooke braced herself for his response, half afraid of what he would do. Would she get the cold politeness of Laney?

"Brooke Palmer," he said in a low, deep voice that to her was as sweet as hot maple syrup drizzling on warm pancakes. It sent a thrill through her; no one said her name the way he did. He didn't seem surprised to see her and gestured to one of the chairs inside the house. "Sit down," he said, walking past her and taking off his hat.

"Thanks." Brooke took a seat and fought not to stare. Without his hat, his brown eyes were clear, reminding her of Montana oil—dark and rich. He was better than the finest wine. And he also got sexier with age.

"I'm sorry about your father."

Brooke blinked, touched by the compassion in his eyes. She forced herself to focus on her reason for coming. Her father had died suddenly and he was the main reason she was there. "Thanks."

"How's Meredith?"

She paused, surprised he'd even ask. "She's in New York with Richard." He was her second husband, but Brooke didn't mention that, not sure Jameson would care.

"I'm glad."

Brooke furrowed her brows in confusion. This wasn't the reaction she'd expected. Who was this even-tempered, controlled man? The Jameson of the past had been more passionate. Especially with her sister. Brooke remembered overhearing an argument they'd had when her sister was preparing to go to college. She had been passing by the family room when she had heard them.

"I don't want to be without you," Meredith had said near tears.

"You know my place is here."

"It doesn't have to be. You're good at so many things. Why can't you attend college in the East with me?"

"I told you what I plan to do."

"You need to stretch your horizons. Get away from farming—"

"You know I'm not just a farmer. You say that just to annoy me."

"I'm trying to find your sense of humor."

"I don't joke about the ranch."

"That's the problem. You already sound like an old man and you haven't even reached twenty yet. Why do you take things so seriously? You don't need to work so hard. You have enough money and the ranch basically runs itself."

"By itself?" he said in surprise. "You talk about the ranch like it's some toy that runs on batteries. Do you know how much it costs to get a cow bred? Or fed? How about vet expenses? And then there are the chickens and—"

"Your family has more than enough money to take care of all of that, and you know it."

"It's not about money. It's about business and I'm going to run it well. For the sake of my family and the sake of our children. Meredith, you know I love you and I will provide the best for us. But my place is here. I like being my own boss and living my life by my rules."

"You mean your family's rules," she snapped.

"They've served me well. This is home."

But, back then, Brooke knew her sister hadn't felt the same about ranching and the land when she was dating him, although she'd pretended she did. Early on, Meredith had always wanted to get away from Granger and thought she could persuade Jameson to do the same. Meredith didn't understand Jameson the way Brooke did. Her sister didn't know how much her teasing words hurt him. As she listened to the argument, Brooke had wanted to run into the room and tell Jameson how much she knew he loved his ranch and his family, and that, if he'd have her, she'd never leave him. But at that time, just like now, he didn't see her in that way. And now she hoped she could change that.

"So what can I do for you?" Jameson asked, his deep voice pulling Brooke out of her memory.

Everything, she wanted to say. For a moment she didn't know herself anymore. She didn't know how to behave with him. She was no longer the awkward girl of fifteen, and he certainly wasn't twenty-two. He was older, a little harder, almost a stranger to her, despite his welcome and patience. But, in spite of her apprehension she knew he was a man she could trust.

"Brooke?"

"I'm sorry," she said quickly, shifting in her seat. "I was just wondering how to say this."

"Don't think about it—just say it."

She gripped her hands in her lap and met his eyes. "I want you to marry me."

Chapter 3

Jameson didn't move. He didn't smile or frown or give any indication of how her request had affected him. He just looked at her with an inscrutable expression.

Brooke gripped her hands tighter. She couldn't have thought he'd get on his knees and propose, although she'd dreamed of a moment like that many times. She didn't know what she'd expected, but it hadn't been this. She could take him being outraged, shocked or even appalled, but his dark steady gaze held her paralyzed. She didn't know if that was a good sign or not. She'd said what she'd wanted and she knew she needed to explain but she didn't know how.

"I know this seems crazy," she said in a rush, desperate to fill the silence. "But I don't know who else to ask. After my father's death things just went—well, I don't know the right word for it really. Then the will was read and he has this requirement in it. And the creditors are knocking down the door and I don't know where else to turn and—"

Jameson crossed the room, sat down beside her and rested his big, firm hands on her shoulders. "Breathe."

Instead she stopped breathing, the feel of his hands seeming to burn through the cloth of her thin cotton jacket, his nearness leaving her weak and unable to move. "I've forgotten how."

A tiny smile softened his mouth. "Brooke, it'll be okay."

She wanted to believe him; she had to. The alternative was too painful. Brooke took a deep breath, knowing that fainting at his feet would only annoy him. "All right."

He searched her eyes. "Good. Now tell me what's going on. Start from the beginning."

"Meredith and I had expected to inherit the ranch."

"But you won't?" he asked when she lowered her gaze.

Brooke licked her lips, wondering if he was even aware that his hands were still on her shoulders. They anchored her, making her feel less alone. With her father gone and her sister away she had no family to turn to. "Dad put a strange codicil in the will. He stipulated that we must *both* be married *before* the ranch can be passed on to us. Because Meredith is married, she's eligible to get her half."

Jameson sat back and released her. It was as if the sound of her sister's name built an instant barrier between them. "But Meredith has no interest in ranch life."

Brooke met his gaze. "I know, and she's been approached by a private broker who is offering her a fortune to sell her half." Ironic as it sounded, Brooke knew she couldn't do that because her father stipulated that in order to inherit the ranch they both had to be married. The only solution Brooke had been able to come up with was that once she was married she would buy out her sister's half.

"What happens if you don't marry?" Jameson asked.

Brooke sighed. "The ranch will remain with Mitch, our ranch foreman." Mitch Stokel had been at her father's side for years. He was trustworthy and a hard worker. "Daddy feared that I wouldn't be able to run the ranch on my own, and he's right."

"Then what's the rush? You're a beautiful woman. You'll have no trouble finding a husband when you're ready."

He thinks I'm beautiful! Brooke had to bite back a smile of satisfaction. She knew she was attractive, and she had grown used to male attention. But Jameson's was the only one that mattered to her. If he liked her looks, did that also mean he was attracted to her? "I don't have time to wait. In the will he also stipulated that if I'm not married within thirty days of the reading of the will, ownership of the ranch will legally pass over to Mitch. I'll be allowed to stay on the ranch as long as I live, and I'll receive a handsome share of the profit if Mitch ever decides to sell, but the ranch won't be mine. And, as I said, Meredith is anxious to get her hands on her half so that she can make money from it. I don't know why he wrote the will the way he did. It seems as if it was his strange way of making sure both his daughters would be married. I don't understand."

Jameson rubbed his chin and frowned. "This has to be illegal. It's blackmail. Have you gotten an attorney to—"

"I've had my attorneys look the will over and it's ironclad. I think, odd though it may seem, my father did this to help me." As a child, Brooke had always been more expressive than Meredith about how much she didn't want to stay on the ranch when she grew up. Although she knew her way around, she'd always been more interested in pursuing her art. She made Western-style pottery. She knew her father didn't want her to feel burdened or obligated. She suspected he felt guilty that the pressure he'd put on his daughters had driven Meredith away. But as she grew Brooke's feelings had changed. She wished now that she had told her father, before he died, how much she had come to love the ranch.

"I know how much your father loved you," Jameson said. "Ray Palmer was a person I admired and a savvy businessman. But this codicil still makes no sense. Why not just let you sell the place? Forcing his daughters to get married in order to keep their own land that they have rightfully inherited makes no sense."

Brooke had asked herself the same question, and she still didn't know the answer. Perhaps it had to do with her father's loneliness. Her mother had died when Brooke was five, and her father had never remarried.

Maybe by stipulating they both get married, he wanted to make sure that she and her sister didn't wind up alone. They had been close to their father. He was their life and had always made sure they were provided for. At times spoiling them more than guiding them.

Brooke remembered the many summers the two of them spent going down the Blackfoot River in an inner tube with him. One of the favorite things she liked to do with her father was fly-fishing. Although he wasn't much of a talker, she simply loved being in his presence. He was a good teacher and was always patient, even when she wasn't. The last time they had gone fishing together, they had traveled up the mountain to a stream where he loved to go. Just to get away. On that trip she had caught a bounty of fish. He had been overjoyed and had congratulated her.

"So, I am a means to an end?" Jameson asked, breaking her reverie.

Brooke blushed. He would be a dream come true, but she couldn't' tell him that. She hoped that her story and situation would be persuasive enough. He was an honorable man. "Like I said, I couldn't think of any other way out of this, and you were the first person I thought of."

Jameson stood and grabbed his hat. "I can't help you. I can't be your fake husband." He was polite, but it was still a rejection.

Brooke should have expected his response, but it was still devastating. Her heart shriveled a little. She understood. He had a life and he didn't want it tied to hers. "I know it's a lot to ask of you, but I'll lose everything. And the implications are bigger than you think.

Mitch has already been talking to the broker who represents Samara Lionne and she's interested in buying Meredith's half of the property. It won't be long before Samara Lionne owns half of Granger. I have to do something now."

Jameson paused. *Samara Lionne?* The same Hollywood starlet who'd bought Wes's property? To hear that woman's name twice in one day wasn't a good sign. "What does she need with a second ranch?"

"Second?"

Jameson set his hat down. "Yes. Wes sold his parcel of land to her. What could she be up to?"

"I don't know. But there is one thing I do know, and that is if I don't get married the entire ranch goes to Mitch, and I'm afraid he'll sell."

This changed everything. At first when she'd talked about getting married, he'd thought it was a joke. A mockery. Did she really think he would marry her? Hell, he didn't even feel like dating. He wasn't ready to think of marriage, let alone marrying the little sister of the woman who left him. Besides, it didn't make sense. Brooke could easily get any man she wanted and probably a host of those she didn't. When he'd first seen her today, it wasn't her mane of wild curls or her hazel eyes that caught his eye; it was her shy smile.

As strikingly beautiful as she was, a man would expect a coy or sexy expression, not something shy and unassuming, almost sweet. Few things in his life were sweet, but Brooke Palmer's grin definitely was. It stirred something in him. When he had turned to look at her, he had been surprised to see her, and he was a little glad, too, although he didn't know why. He'd always liked her. As a child she seemed to appear at the strangest times, when he was roping or returning the cattle to the pen, and always with her little sketch pad. He didn't mind her presence; she was never a bother or in his way.

He wanted to help her, but he didn't want to marry her. He didn't plan to marry anyone. His focus was on BWB, but based on what she'd told him he understood her desperation. He didn't want her to lose her land. Those facts united them in a way he hadn't imagined. She understood what was at stake.

Brooke stood. "I'm sorry for disturbing you."

Jameson stopped her. At first he'd thought her idea ridiculous, but he suddenly realized that her request wasn't about romance or other fleeting emotions. This was a business deal. This was about saving history, their heritage. She understood it as much as he did. He met her startled hazel gaze. She really had grown into a beautiful woman. For a moment she made him think of the Calliope hummingbird—swift and bright. It was common to Montana and its name came from the Greek word meaning "little star." With a woman like Brooke he could accomplish his goal. He was tired of outsiders messing with his town and interfering with the privacy they'd been able to maintain for generations. She wanted to use him, and he could use her. It would make them equals. A team.

"Brooke," he said. "You've got yourself a groom." He extended his hand to her. She took it and quickly let go.

* * *

Brooke wanted to hug him, kiss him, dance, maybe even laugh, but instead she rocked on her heels and hugged herself. "Great. We can go to the justice of the peace or just elope."

Jameson shook his head. "If we're going to do this, we'll do it big."

Her arms fell to her sides. "Big?"

"Yes, the bigger the better. Our wedding is going to be one this town will remember. We need to make a symbolic statement and show everyone that the families of Granger stick together." His eyes were serious and probing. "Are you sure you want to do this?"

Brooke met his dark stare. He was giving her a chance to turn back and retain her dignity. He was offering her a warning that he wouldn't be an easy man to marry, that his heart belonged to the BWB. Not her. But, instead of being uneasy, her resolve grew. Even if their marriage would just be for show, it would be a dream come true for her to walk down the aisle toward Jameson Broward. She knew she was taking a big gamble, but she didn't care.

"Brooke?" Jameson repeated. "Are you sure you're ready for this?"

She smiled. "With all my heart." She was sure.

Chapter 4

Jameson was sure his mother hadn't blinked for a full minute. His father just stared at him and then finally said, "You're doing what?"

The three of them sat in the Great Room, where only yesterday they'd been discussing Wes's property sale. "I'm getting married," Jameson said.

"To Brooke Palmer?" Gwendolyn repeated, just to make sure she'd heard her son correctly the first time.

He nodded. "Yes. We're getting married this month."

"But you can't be serious," Gwendolyn said.

"I am. You know I don't joke."

"But Brooke is—"

"I know who she is," he cut in, not wanting his mother to elaborate. "How I feel about her shocked me, too, but

I can't help it. We've been seeing each other for some time."

"How long?"

"Long enough for me to know I want to marry her."

"But it's so sudden," Steven said. "Why not wait?"

"I don't want to wait. I asked and she accepted and that's all there is to it."

"Really?" Steven said, doubtful.

Gwendolyn frowned. "You know how this will look?"

Jameson couldn't help a grin. "I plan to make it look spectacular, and I need your help. Brooke has no one to help her so I said I'd take care of everything, but since I don't know much about weddings…" He let his words fade away and sent his mother a look of hope.

"You want me to organize everything," Gwendolyn finished.

"With no expense spared."

And he meant every word. So Gwendolyn went into "planning" mode, and before he knew it, a lavish wedding was quickly set into motion. She had their wedding invitations designed. She also put together a list of dignitaries and guests she knew absolutely had to be there and other lesser-known ones, just so that they didn't feel snubbed. A wedding planner was hired to assist with the overall organization and all related events including interviewing a number of caterers. Brooke thought she would be able to get to do some things on her own, like select her dress, but Gwendolyn insisted on helping her select her wedding gown.

"No daughter-in-law of mine is going to wear an

off-the-rack dress." And she was good to her word. She flew Brooke, along with Laney, in a private plane to Atlanta, Georgia, where Gwendolyn had made an appointment with a top fashion designer to make a custom wedding dress for Brooke. It was stunning. It had a bare back that plunged just enough to be both revealing and modest, with transparent, off-the-shoulder sleeves that extended into beaded gloves and a cinched, gathered waist, with a long train and a full billowy embroidered silk skirt that accentuated Brooke's drop-dead figure.

News of Brooke and Jameson's engagement spread through Granger overnight, like wildfire. But, the closer they came to the actual date, the more concerned his family became. Although his mother no longer expressed her doubts and his grandfather kept whatever thoughts he had to himself, his father was more to the point. One late afternoon, Steven visited his son as Jameson went over some paperwork in his study.

"You sure you know what you're doing marrying this woman?" Steven asked.

Jameson sniffed, more amused than offended by the question. "I always know what I'm doing."

His father sat. "That's what worries me."

"Why?"

"Because I feel as if you're up to something. You can try to fool the rest of the family with your story about having a clandestine relationship, but I know you too well. I also know when I see a man in love and from what I've seen, that isn't you."

Jameson pushed his paperwork aside and rested his

arms on the desk, prepared for a fight he planned to win. "I care about her."

"You 'care' about your cattle, but when it comes to loving a woman, you need to feel a little bit more than that." Steven folded his arms. "I know she loves you." He smiled when he saw Jameson flinch. "Why does that surprise you?"

Because you're wrong, Jameson wanted to say. He had to admire Brooke. She was playing her role as his fiancée better than he'd expected. "I didn't say it did."

"A look passed your face. If you don't plan on accepting her love how can you give it back?"

"I'll take good care of her."

"There's that word again. Care. Don't shame me and Ray Palmer, but most of all, don't shame her. If this is your idea of some sort of twisted revenge against Meredith, I want you to stop it."

"It's not. That happened more than ten years ago. I'm over it."

"Are you?"

Jameson leaned back in his chair. "It's not like you to ask me to repeat myself."

"You two were inseparable in school. When she left you…" He sighed and cleared his throat, as if the topic embarrassed him. "We all know how devastated you were because you loved her so much."

"Don't talk to me about love," Jameson said in a tight voice. "I know all about love and what it can do. My feelings for Meredith are strong and deep. She and I are getting married and I don't have to defend myself against you."

"Brooke," Steven corrected in a soft tone.

"What?"

"You just said you were marrying Meredith."

Jameson felt heat rush to his face, but he kept his gaze steady. He couldn't back down now. "I meant Brooke."

"Really? You think making a mistake like that is something trivial?"

Jameson sighed, annoyed by his slip. "No."

"I hope you're marrying Brooke for the right reasons."

"I am."

"Don't throw away a lot of money on a gamble you plan to lose."

"You know I don't like to lose, so why would I start now?"

But Jameson already knew he had won. Yes, he was helping her, but she was also helping him. But was marrying Brooke a way to avenge himself? Was he ready to be Meredith's brother-in-law? He'd be rebuilding a bond that had been broken, but it was a strategic tactic he believed his family would eventually understand and respect. However, his father was right—he didn't love her. But Brooke didn't love him either. His father was mistaken. It was gratitude he'd sensed, not love. But there was no need to tell him the truth.

Unfortunately, Jameson knew his father knew him too well, and his mother, too. He had to act more like the loving fiancé and later, husband, if he wanted to keep the questions at bay. He was pleased that his actions had alleviated some of the earlier worry they had about the selling of Granger land. He didn't want them concerned about what Samara was up to. Maybe they should have just eloped, but no, that wasn't his style. He had to let people know that the Browards were on the defensive. They hadn't built a fortune by laying low. He wouldn't be like his brother and disappear when it was time to fight.

That evening, Jameson went to the Shank of the Evening saloon in downtown Granger to clear his head. He could take the curiosity of the town more than his family's suspicions. Even his house manager, Cecelia, had had something to say about his upcoming wedding.

"The town is just buzzing about your wedding," she said one evening as she cleared up Jameson's dinner dishes. Her spiky red hair matched her ruddy cheeks and hinted at her Irish heritage. "It will be nice to have a woman around the house."

Jameson picked up a magazine. "I thought you were enough."

"You know what I mean."

Her green eyes twinkled. "You are a sly one, seeing a woman on the side without anyone knowing."

"Hmm…"

"But I'm surprised some woman hadn't set her sights on you and reeled you in earlier."

Jameson flipped through the magazine, used to Cecelia's chatter. "Yes."

"However, it does seem rather sudden. Is she?"

Jameson stopped and looked at her. "Is she what?"

"Expecting."

"Expecting what?"

Her face reddened. "Don't be stupid. You know what I'm talking about."

Jameson cupped his chin and studied her. "Do I really look like the kind of man who'd get himself into that kind of trouble?"

"No, but—"

Jameson grinned and lifted his paper. He didn't mind her questions. Cecelia was one of the few people he felt he could trust. She knew his ways and habits and gave him space when he wanted it. "There's your answer."

"I'm glad. But I hope you don't wait too long to fill this big house with children."

Jameson stopped listening to her after that. There would be no children, not for a long time.

At the bar Jameson sighed at the memory of Cecelia's hopeful chatter, ordered a drink then took it outside to watch the traffic—what little there was of it—go by. He sat down, balanced his chair back on two legs and pushed his hat down low, ready to relax. Within seconds he saw a shapely pair of legs stop in front of him.

Jameson heard the distinct sound of a camera lens coming into focus. "I don't want to make you regret taking that picture," he said.

He heard a gasp of surprise and hid a grin.

"Not even just one?" a feminine voice said.

Jameson pushed his hat back and looked up. The voice belonged to a citified version of a Southern belle, from the French twist in her hair to her expensive leather heels. "No."

"It's just that I've never seen a real live cowboy before."

"How do you know I am one?"

"You look the part."

He sighed. Most people were as shallow as a dried-up creek. "Looks can be deceiving."

The attractive lady lifted her camera and flashed a flirty grin. "Come on, just one little picture as a souvenir."

"I'm being polite now, but I can be mean. I can guarantee you don't want to see that side of me."

Something in his tone wiped the smile from her face. The woman tucked her camera away in the large designer bag slung over her shoulder and hurried to her car.

Jameson raised his glass, as if offering a silent toast of victory, then took a drink, wishing he could get rid of all the outsiders as easily.

"Don't you think you're laying the surly cowboy act on a bit too thick?" Brooke said behind him.

Jameson stiffened, annoyed that the sound of her voice sent a fissure of awareness through him, then he quickly recovered himself. "It's not an act. It's how I am."

Brooke sat down in front of him. "You weren't always like that."

"I've changed."

"Me, too."

He lifted a brow, doubtful.

"I've gotten older, in case you haven't noticed."

"I've noticed." *A little more than I want to.* He sipped

his drink and looked around. This place was more Wes's scene than his. If he'd really wanted to be left alone, he should have gone for a ride. Yes, a long trek up one of the mountains would have been a better option. Instead of having to listen to the sound of raucous music emanating from the saloon and being bothered by uninvited women on the street.

"Dance with me."

Jameson took a long swallow, his gaze focused on the street. "Why?"

"People are already talking. I think we should add more chapters to this story."

Jameson finished his drink and set the glass down. "I don't dance."

"I can teach you."

He stood. "Bye."

"Don't you think we should have one date before we get married?"

Jameson looked at her confused. "Date?"

"Yes. We should at least show people that we're a couple."

"They'll know for sure the moment you walk down the aisle. I have nothing to prove."

"Please."

Jameson studied her for a moment. She was being sincere and he knew he was disappointing her, but he didn't dance well and he wasn't going to make a fool of himself for anyone. Besides, he was tired. He'd gotten up at four in the morning and it had been a long day. But she was right, they should give the town something to talk about. And he needed to show his father that marrying Brooke wasn't some twisted plot of revenge. He looked inside the bar then thought of an idea. "Darts."

Brooke frowned. "What?"

"You once asked me to teach you how to throw darts."

Brooke threw up her hands in apparent exasperation. "Jameson, that was *years* ago. I must have been twelve."

"Well, I'm ready to teach you." He grabbed her wrist, pulled her inside and headed over to the dartboard.

Jameson patiently told her the rules of the game, then showed her how to hold the dart and aim. "It takes practice, but it's fun. Now you try."

Brook took a dart, threw it with the skill of a champion and hit the bull's-eye. "You mean like this?" She threw another dart, again hitting dead center. "Or like this?" She threw it a third time. "Or maybe like this."

Jameson rested his hands on his hips. "I didn't realize I was such a good teacher," he said in a dry tone.

Brooke laughed, pleased that he didn't mind her teasing. "I couldn't wait around for you, so I found someone else to teach me."

"Who?"

"You wouldn't know him."

"Him?"

"Does that make a difference?"

"No."

Brooke wished it did. She wanted him to be curious, even a little jealous, but he wasn't. Jameson left after giving her a quick peck on the lips, just for show. Maybe she shouldn't have shown off. She liked having him trying to teach her. She remembered her back pressing against his chest. The feel of his strong hand steadying her arm. She didn't blame the lady visitor for wanting to take a picture of him. He may not appreciate attention from the fairer sex, but he certainly encouraged it without effort. He was a fine specimen of a man.

Someone tapped her on the shoulder. She turned and saw a waitress holding out a tray with a drink. "This is for you. It's from the man over there."

Brooke turned and saw Mitch grinning at her. She took the drink and walked over to his table. "What's this for?"

"I thought you'd need the courage to keep this charade up."

"Charade?"

Mitch nodded to the dartboard. "That was quite a show you two put on, but it won't work."

"What are you talking about?"

"I know this engagement thing is a fake, and if your marriage lasts longer than a week, I'll eat my hat."

Brooke smiled, pressing back a sense of unease. "Good. I'll be there to grill it for you."

He couldn't stop thinking about her. Jameson went to bed in a nasty mood and woke up in an even meaner one. He couldn't stop thinking about the sly grin Brooke had given him at the bar after hitting three bull's-eyes. Each time he felt as if she were aiming at his heart. No, not his heart, much lower than that and to a much more delicate part of his anatomy. He'd been turned on by the shape of her butt in her tight-fitting jeans and the feel of her soft skin under his fingers as he taught her how to hold and throw a dart. He could still smell her perfume.

He'd gotten too close, but he wouldn't make that mistake again. He had to stay away from her. Unfortunately, Brooke didn't give him the opportunity. She showed up on the ranch the next day while he was busying himself looking over some of the calves.

"I forgot to tell you something."

Jameson stiffened. *Wasn't marrying her enough?* "What?"

"It's about my studio."

He felt himself relax and returned his gaze to the herd. "What about it?" he asked absently as his gaze focused on a calf that looked listless. Not a good sign.

"I need one. Can I have a space in your house?"

"Hmm."

"Jameson, are you listening to me? It's important that I have the space I need."

"You'll get it," he said, noticing another calf that didn't look healthy. It wasn't playing or running like the others. "Excuse me."

"What's wrong?" Brooke asked, following close behind him.

He walked over to the calf and pointed. "Tell me what you see."

"She doesn't look good."

Jameson silently swore. They'd had a great calving season, but it was still a delicate time for the newborn calves. He had to keep constant watch for broken bones from being stomped on by the herd or for infections. He still felt bad about the call from his foreman, telling him he'd lost a horse he'd hoped to rescue and the second one was still touch and go. He didn't need more bad news. He walked over and pulled the skin on one of the calf's necks. It lacked the elasticity he expected, meaning it was dehydrated. He watched Brooke do the same with another calf.

"This one is dehydrated, but I don't see any of the others looking as bad."

Jameson called over a ranch hand, Frank, and they checked the calves' body temperatures. They were running too hot. "Separate these two," he told Frank. "And you know the rest." Jameson and Frank knew they'd need to get the fluids the vet had provided to the calves quickly in order not to lose them.

"Brooke," Jameson said with a note of apology. "We'll talk about the studio later. Okay?"

"No problem."

The following day the calves were doing much better, but Jameson's mood hadn't improved much. He kept thinking about Brooke checking the calf for dehydration. She'd sprung into action without him asking her or telling her what needed to be done. It had felt good to have her at his side…too good. He couldn't afford to feel this way. He had to think business. He called his lawyer. "I need you to do something for me. Fast."

The next day Jameson sat in Brooke's front room with a legal prenuptial agreement and a pen ready. It was two days before their wedding, and he wanted to get something settled. "I need you to read this agreement, then sign," he said more brusquely than he meant to.

Brooke lifted the papers. "What is it?"

"A business agreement. This will protect you as much as it does me."

She set the papers down. "I don't need to sign."

"If you want this marriage to go through, you will."

"I don't want anything from you except to save my legacy."

"Then sign and there won't be a problem." He knew that people's intentions could change. He was sure she meant well now, but he'd been burned before, and he wouldn't make the same mistake of trusting a woman twice. "This is strictly business. As your father stipulated in his will, we have to stay married for at least a year. After that we'll part ways and you'll get your ranch."

"You certainly know how to make a girl feel wanted. I'll sign, but you can't keep treating our relationship this way."

"What way?"

"Like we're business colleagues."

Jameson nodded, pleased with the description. "That's essentially what we are."

Brooke lowered her voice, although no one was around to overhear. "Only *we* know that, but others can't think so. If I sign this, I need you to play the part of my husband. A devoted husband."

Jameson shrugged with nonchalance. "I can do that."

"Prove it."

"I did. In the saloon—"

"You treated me like your kid sister," Brooke interrupted. "Not your fiancée. Mitch is already laughing about how fake this engagement looks and he's sharing his opinions. What does your family think?"

"I guess you have a point," Jameson agreed with reluctance. "Okay. I promise I'll play the role so you get to keep your family homestead." He held the pen out.

Brooke shook her head. "I said *prove* it."

Jameson looked around. "Why? Nobody's watching."

"Then it's a good time to practice, don't you think?"

"Practice what?"

"Being a husband."

Jameson waved the pen. "And you won't sign until I do?"

Brooke crossed her legs and sat back with a satisfied grin. "That's right."

"Quite a negotiation tactic, but you have a lot more to lose than I do."

"I grew up with a rancher, I know that most things in life are a gamble. One just needs to weigh his or her options."

"When you gamble you should make sure the odds are in your favor. What makes you think I'll do what you ask? What will you do if I say no?"

Her grin widened. "You won't."

"You sound sure about that."

"I am because I know you like a challenge as much as I do."

Jameson raised his brows. "You think you know me well?"

"Am I right?"

He folded his arms. "Okay, so you want me to act like your husband?"

"Devoted," Brooke added with emphasis. "Convince me that I'm yours."

"That shouldn't be hard."

"Let me see you try."

"I don't 'try.' I succeed."

"So far you're all talk."

"You're right."

Jameson didn't move. His arms remained folded. He didn't move closer, but the air suddenly became still and charged with an electric heat like the coming of lightning. Brooke felt her throat grow dry as his gaze lazily appraised her in a way that was both intimate and naughty. His eyes undressed her. She suddenly felt lightheaded. But just as quickly as the expression came it disappeared and his face turned into a bland mask.

"Did you find that convincing?" he said in a flat tone.

Brooke could only nod, her mind spinning. She wanted to "practice" some more, but she wasn't bold enough to ask him to. She'd been surprised she'd been able to get him to show false affection even once.

Jameson handed her the pen, a smile hovering over his lips. "Ready to say 'I do'?"

Brooke took the pen from him, with slightly trembling fingers. She'd been ready for years.

Chapter 5

He dreamed about her that night. Jameson hadn't dreamed about a woman in years. Usually around this time of the year he was focused on making sure the machines they used for feeding the cattle were in order. Instead, he replayed the sight of Brooke sitting in her front room, daring him to act like a devoted husband. He could tell by the flush on her cheeks that he'd made his point, but he'd burned himself in the process. He'd let himself imagine her riding on a horse, naked with her wild hair covering her like a Midwestern Lady Godiva. Then he pictured her naked with her hair pulled back so he could clearly see the curves of her body, her breasts and… He swore. The problem was he shouldn't have pictured her naked at all.

That wasn't part of the bargain. He had to take the

lead in this. He had to be responsible. She trusted him. Jameson pounded his pillow then stared at the far wall. He didn't trust closing his eyes yet. It must be all the wedding preparation that had gotten him off his game. It had altered his train of thought. Once he was married things would return to normal. For now, all that mattered was keeping Brooke's ranch.

She dreamed about him that night, but it wasn't like any dream Brooke ever had of Jameson before. Her mind didn't wander to white dresses and wedding rings. She didn't think about walking down the aisle or holding his hand. No, she didn't dream the dreams of a young girl, but that of a woman. A woman whose secret love for a man had turned into something more. Something even she had never envisioned. Something raw, wild and thrilling. In her dream she made that brief look of lust that had entered his gaze real. She made him want her in a way he'd never craved a woman. She made his eyes fill with a passion so intense that he vowed he would never let her go. And in her dream, he saw her as more than just a challenge or even a possession. She was his true desire. Not her sister or the BWB, just her.

Mitch was about to take a nap on the wraparound porch of the Palmer property when he saw a sight he never expected to see: Steven Broward walking up the drive.

Mitch stood up. "Can I help you?"

"Yes," Steven said as he took a seat next to him. "Tell me what you know."

Mitch hesitated. "About what?"

"Brooke. And don't pretend you don't know what I'm talking about. You've been spreading rumors about her relationship with my son."

"I wasn't spreading rumors."

"You don't think it's real and neither do I. Did you ever see them together?"

"No, but I'm usually working. She's not my daughter to look after."

"Do you know of any reason why this marriage shouldn't go through?"

"No, sir."

Steven was quiet for a long moment then said, "If you change your mind, you know how to reach me."

Mitch nodded, but Steven didn't move.

"Is there something else?" Mitch asked.

"Yes, has anyone been asking you about this property?"

"You should ask Brooke about that."

"Don't try to BS me, Mitch. We both know you know a lot more about what goes on around the Palmer homestead than she does."

It was a truth Mitch couldn't deny, even though at that moment he wanted to. "Yes, there's been interest from buyers but that's no different than what others here in Granger are saying."

"What are they saying?"

Mitch shrugged. "Just that it might be time to sell and move on."

"You're not telling me much."

"Because there's not much to say, really. I don't know

who the buyers are, just that they represent people, I don't know how many, with a lot of money to throw around." Mitch couldn't help a grin. "Something you'd know a lot more about than me."

Steven didn't return the smile. "I would like to know why."

"Why people are selling?"

"No. Who has caused this sudden interest in buying up land in Granger and why."

"Sorry, I can't help you."

Steven sent him a long look. "Nothing about Brooke and Jameson or these 'secret' investors, hmm? You know, there used to be a time when I knew all the land-owners, and we never had to worry about anyone thinking of selling off their land. There was an unwritten rule that the heirs would inherit the land and everything would stay in the family. I guess it was foolish of us to think nothing would change. Even my own son got caught up in this money grabbing."

"Yup. I heard he sold that piece of land he had."

"Do you know to who?" Although he already knew, Steven wanted to bait Mitch to see if he had more information to offer.

"Heard he sold it to that actress somebody, I don't remember her name. Shame, because if I had known he was going to sell it I would have made him an offer."

"So would we. He didn't even let his family know. The younger generation doesn't seem to see the importance of keeping a legacy. They have little or no respect for the hard work and years of sacrifice their ancestors made in order to turn this land into what it is today."

Mitch held out his hands in a helpless gesture. "I wish I could tell you the news you want to hear, but I don't have it."

Steven nodded. "Fine," he said as he stood. He then walked to his car, which was parked at the end of the long driveway.

Mitch let out his breath after Steven had gone. That had been a close call. He didn't want to get on the bad side of a Broward. He walked inside and picked up the framed picture of Ray Palmer that sat on the marble tabletop in the hallway. He missed the man who'd been like a father to him. "You're causing a lot of trouble. I hope you know what you're doing."

The day before the wedding Brooke went into town to shop for some food items for dinner that night. She'd been so busy preparing for the wedding and working in her studio, she hadn't spared much time for going shopping, and her cupboards were bare. She caught a glimpse of the actress Samara Lionne on the other side of the street and again wondered why Granger, of all places, had captured her interest. Brooke looked away; she had her own concerns to think about.

"I can't believe Jameson is actually beating his brother to the aisle," Brooke overheard an older woman say from the next aisle. She recognized the voice as Mrs. Clarksdale, her fourth-grade teacher, a woman who seemed ageless because she'd always looked old. She had wiry gray hair with ice-blue eyes.

"Especially to a Palmer," her friend Mrs. Lanke

replied. A large woman with blond hair and a wide gummy smile, she was married to the local furrier.

"I think she's so lucky," her daughter Reba said. She looked like a younger version of her mother. "He's so handsome."

"That handsome face hides a hard heart," Mrs. Lanke said with certainty. "Everyone knows his only true love is the BWB."

"I feel a little sorry for her," Mrs. Clarksdale said. "He's probably only marrying her because he couldn't get her sister."

"Yes, Jameson is a one-woman man," Mrs. Lanke agreed. "I doubt he'll ever give his heart away again."

"He's marrying her, isn't he?" Reba said.

"A man can marry without the thought of love easier than a woman can. I just hope poor Brooke knows what she's getting into. She's all alone with no one to advise her. Both her parents are dead and her sister is far away in New York. He's probably marrying her just to add a few more acres to what they already own."

"She'll have the Broward millions to keep her warm," Reba replied with a laugh.

"Cash can be cold comfort, no matter how much you have."

"Besides, she's not a gold digger," Mrs. Clarksdale said in a defensive tone. "The Browards wouldn't allow her into the fold if she were. They're the only family she'll have now."

Brooke left the store. Was that how others saw her? As poor Brooke? Did they really think that Jameson was using her? She wanted to tell them that they were wrong about him. That he was a good man. That he was marrying her to help save her inheritance, but she knew she couldn't defend him without revealing the truth. And they were right. He didn't love her and their marriage would be a sham.

A Bride for Broward.
Sorry, ladies, but another Broward man is going off the market. The date is set and the guests are ready. But will the bride show up this time?

Charles Broward set the paper down and laughed. "This is the eighth story I've read about your upcoming wedding. You should see the pictures they have of the two of you online. Not even your father got this much press when he was getting ready to marry your mother."

Jameson grimaced at his grandfather's amusement. "That's only because the internet hadn't been invented yet." The two men sat in the main family room eating their dessert of lemon meringue pie. "I hate reporters."

"You're news now, so get used to it."

"It'll fade. I'm not as interesting as Wes, and that Samara woman gets enough press for all of us."

"True," Charles said, some of his good mood fading.

"I thought you called me over to talk business."

Charles shot him a look. "Life isn't always about work."

Jameson sighed. He respected his grandfather, but he wasn't in the mood for a lecture. "I know that."

"When are you going to start living?"

Jameson set his dessert aside. "I'm living now."

"Then how come there's no mention of a honeymoon?"

"We have a lot of business to take care of right now. There'll be time for that later."

Charles was silent for a moment then said, "I heard the bride is giving herself away."

"You've been hearing a lot of things lately."

"I may be old, but my hearing hasn't faded. Am I right?"

"Yes."

He nodded. "She's got an independent streak. That's good."

"Why?"

Charles smiled then said, "You've finally met your match."

Their wedding came with the sound of singing birds and not a cloud in the sky. Jameson was in his bedroom fighting with his cuff links, the words of his grandfather rattling in his mind. Had he finally met his match? What did he mean? How could Brooke be his match? She was hardly out of college. After their "arranged" year was up, they would get divorced and she would likely move back to her ranch and get someone else to help her and Mitch. His grandfather had it all wrong.

Jameson paused when someone knocked. "Come in."

His brother, Wes, walked into the room and closed the door. He and his fiancée, Lydia, had returned from their European vacation to attend his wedding. Wes looked ready to be his best man with his close-cropped hair and goatee trimmed to perfection. He had a more muscular build and a more carefree attitude than Jameson, but he didn't look carefree now.

"You know this is crazy," Wes said, glaring at Jameson's reflection in the mirror.

"What's crazy about getting married?" Jameson said in a bored tone. In fifteen minutes he had to be in front of the preacher. Everything was on schedule. "You're planning to."

"I won't be doing it so that I can get some land," Wes said.

Jameson spun around to him. "What's that supposed to mean?"

"People have been talking—"

"People are always talking."

"Especially Mitch. No one believes you and Brooke are marrying for love."

"So what?"

"When are you going to learn that people are more important than property?"

Jameson turned back to the mirror. "Funny how you suddenly feel in the mood to offer advice when you never take any."

"You were wrong about Lydia."

Jameson nodded, not too proud to admit it. "True. So, I guess that now makes you an expert on women." He grabbed his jacket off the hanger and put it on. "You want to give me some tips about Brooke?"

"Don't hurt her."

Jameson turned to his brother, at first surprised and then angry, but he kept his voice level. "I don't plan to. *I* don't hurt the people I care about."

"I haven't hurt anyone."

"You weren't around to see Dad's and Grandpa Charles's faces when they heard you'd sold your land. Or to hear Mom ask why you would do so without telling anyone. But that doesn't matter. I forgot, you live by different rules. You're free to do whatever you want."

Wes shook his head. "You're still mad about that? What's the big deal? I didn't want it anymore."

Jameson narrowed his eyes. "You could have sold it to any one of us. Me, for instance."

"I didn't think you needed it."

"I don't think you were thinking at all."

"So what if some Hollywood actress has taken interest in our town?"

Jameson frowned. "She's up to something. But you're too impressed by the glamour that surrounds her to notice. And, I forgot, the money."

"You just don't like outsiders of any kind."

"I hope you don't end up regretting your choice."

Wes turned to the door. "Right back at you, brother."

Jameson's cell phone rang. He glanced at the number and tensed. It was Brooke. Why was she calling him? Was she backing out? Why did he care if she did? At that moment Meredith's call repeated in his mind with agonizing clarity.

"Aren't you going to answer that?" Wes asked, curious when his brother continued to stare at the phone.

Jameson swallowed then connected. "Yes?"

"Jameson?" Brooke said.

"No."

"What?"

"Brooke, why would you call my phone and then ask me that question?"

"Because someone else could have answered. I just wanted to make sure."

"Fine. Yes, it's me." He glanced at his brother then turned and lowered his voice. "Is something wrong?"

"No. I just wanted to say thanks for doing this."

Jameson's heartbeat returned to normal, then he looked at his brother and raised his brows, indicating that he wanted him to go, but Wes just smiled and folded his arms. Jameson curled his lip; his little brother knew how to annoy him. He had to choose his reply carefully. He couldn't say "You're welcome" because that would make Wes suspicious. If he said "Okay," Wes might wonder what the question was. He had to keep his reply vague. He made a noncommittal sound, said, "See you soon," and then hung up.

"Does the bride have cold feet?" Wes teased.

Jameson walked past him and opened the door. "It's too late to replace you as best man, right?"

Wes patted him on the back. "You're starting to develop a sense of humor."

"I wasn't kidding," Jameson said in a tone that made his brother laugh.

The wedding was held on the grounds of the BWB estate. The entire ranch was decorated for the big day. The wedding planner, who had been given an open checkbook for the event, had flown in a French baker to make the wedding cake. She had also hired a well-known interior decorator to create an outdoor wedding chapel made entirely of white and red roses. The guests were all given a small token to take with them—Godiva chocolate, the best handmade peanut brittle in Montana and a fifty-dollar coupon they could redeem at the BWB ranch's gift shop.

Gwendolyn had set the shop up as another source of income. She had discovered that people liked taking a piece of the ranch with them and had secured the talent of several local Native American artists to make artifacts and crafts bearing the Broward Webb Broward Heritage Ranch name.

The wedding brimmed with excitement as a live band played an assortment of musical scores as guests continued to arrive. Although no one from Brooke's family was present, all the Browards were in attendance: Steven; Gwen; Grandpa Charles with his date, Polly Ann Weir, grandmother of the twenty-two-year-old Patti Weir, who'd won him at the bachelor charity auction; Laney; Wes and Lydia. Gwendolyn looked stunning in a designer Italian suit, and Steven wore a matching tuxedo. Laney had chosen to wear a simple but elegant, floor-length taffeta gown. Wes had indulged Lydia with a cream, lace sheath dress that fit her body like a glove. If her outfit had been white, she would have definitely been in competition with the bride, which seemed to those in attendance to be just what she had in mind. Once the groom's family was seated, the minister took his position behind the pulpit, Jameson and Wes took their positions and the band began playing the wedding march.

As Brooke walked down the aisle, she noticed Jameson's quick intake of breath. Then she saw a small smile when her hand-tooled cowboy boots peeked from beneath her dress. He seemed to like what he was seeing. Then she looked at Gwendolyn. The older woman smiled, but Brooke wasn't sure if it was from pity or welcome. She hoped it was the latter. The Browards were now her new family, at least for a time, and she desperately wanted a place where she belonged.

When she reached Jameson's side, Brooke suddenly realized that there was no turning back, but she didn't want to. Soon they exchanged rings and spoke their vows and then the pastor announced, "You may kiss the bride."

Jameson leaned close and whispered, "I'll make it look good if you will." Then he planted a heart-stopping kiss on her lips. Brooke could hardly hear the shouts of congratulations and had to stop herself from leaning in closer for more.

Her lips still burned from his kiss moments later when Brooke threw her bouquet. It flew through the air over the many women vying for it and fell directly in Laney's lap, the only single woman who hadn't left her seat to catch it. Laney glanced down at the flowers then burst into tears and ran from the reception. Unfortunately, because all eyes were focused on them, Brooke was unable to go after her. Instead, she stayed by her new husband's side as they circulated and began meeting their guests.

The reception was held under a massive white tent with a wooden dance floor. But Brooke still couldn't convince Jameson to dance.

"Please," Brooke said, a little desperate. "Everyone expects it."

Jameson suddenly grabbed his leg then winced.

"What's wrong?"

"I think I pulled a muscle."

"Boy, you better dance with your bride or I'll really give you a reason to wince," Steven said, overhearing their conversation.

Jameson groaned, took Brooke's hand and led her to the middle of the dance floor with as much joy as a calf being roped. The musical ensemble quickly changed to play the song that Brooke had selected. Jameson pulled her in close to him and began dancing with a smooth rhythm that stunned her. Brooke became aware of how sleekly muscled he was, the scent of his cologne and the powerful way he moved.

"I thought you said you couldn't dance," Brooke said, sounding more breathy than she wanted to. She had to act nonchalant. She didn't want him to know how much he affected her.

"I never said that," he said, his voice a deep rumble. "I said I *don't* dance, not that I can't dance."

"You should do it more often." She smiled up at him, eager to cross the chasm that still separated them. Just because their marriage was false didn't mean they couldn't have some fun. "Especially now that you have someone to dance with."

"I'd rather play darts."

Brooke laughed, although his admission that he'd rather play darts than dance with her hurt. "Your ego can take me beating you?"

Jameson only smiled.

* * *

From across the room Steven sat alone at his table and watched the couple. His wife had pulled off a miracle. The wedding had been perfect, but something about Jameson and Brooke bothered him.

"What are you thinking?" Charles asked, taking a seat next to him.

"Nothing."

"The father of the groom shouldn't look so suspicious. What's on your mind?"

Steven looked around. "Where's your lady friend?"

"Powdering her nose. Now stop avoiding my question."

"I'm thinking what everyone else is probably asking themselves. What the hell is going on here?"

"A wedding," Charles said. "There's nothing more to it."

Steven looked at his father, amused. "You don't believe it."

"I want to believe it."

"But you have doubts."

"Jameson is a smart young man. I guess I have more faith in your son than you do." He nodded to the pair. "They make a handsome couple."

"That's not what makes a marriage last."

"You caused quite a stir in your day. People wondered why you were *really* marrying Gwendolyn and look at the two of you now."

"Did you have your doubts?"

"Does that matter now?"

"Right." Steven sighed. "I should trust him, but what

worries me is that he'd go for a Palmer of all the women out there."

Charles shrugged. "When it comes to love, the heart knows no reason."

Steven shook his head. "Jameson is not a romantic. Those two are up to something and I'm going to find out what it is."

"It's a done deal. Leave it alone."

Steven didn't reply. He still had a few questions he wanted to get answered.

"That's an order, not a suggestion," Charles said, as if he'd read his son's thoughts. "Leave them alone."

Steven lifted his glass and nodded.

After Jameson and Brooke finished their first dance, the floor filled with guests of all ages, from two-year-olds to octogenarians, including Grandpa Charles and his date. A catering company out of Helena had prepared a magnificent feast consisting of lobster tail, shrimp cocktail and baby back ribs in heavy spiced sauce. As for drinks, wine and beer flowed freely throughout the night and into the early morning.

Late in the evening, after the traditional toasts and ceremonial cake cutting, and the highlight, the removal of Brooke's garter belt, Brooke and Jameson made their exit, leaving the guests to party in their absence. "Are you sure we should be leaving so soon?" Brooke asked as Jameson led her to his car.

"They won't miss us. Besides, let the rumors fly as to what we're really up to."

Brooke felt mixed emotions as they drove back to his

house. She was still shaken from his kiss. It was now official. She was Mrs. Jameson Broward. Since she was fifteen she had dreamed of this moment, but knowing the conditions under which he had married her, Brooke knew it was just business to him. If only she could feel the same. Although she knew there would be no honeymoon, she had hoped to stay and enjoy their wedding just a little longer.

The day had started with Brooke being picked up by a taxi early in the morning and being driven to the Browards' main house, at Gwendolyn's insistence. Brooke had been put in one of their special suites, reserved for important guests, all set to be pampered, beginning with a sumptuous breakfast. Following breakfast, Gwendolyn's manicurist had come over and given Brooke a full manicure and pedicure, which was then followed by a full-body massage, which she needed to help keep her anxiety at bay. Gwendolyn's hairstylist then arrived late in the morning to style Brooke's hair before the makeup artist added the finishing touches.

"You know you are part of our family now," Gwendolyn had said as she entered the suite once everyone had left. "And I want you to wear these on your special day." She opened a small rectangular jewelry box, revealing a pair of exquisitely designed twenty-four-carat gold earrings encrusted with rubies. "These belonged to my mother and her mother before her. Now I'm giving them to you."

"But…"

"No buts. Remember you need to wear something old as well as something new." After helping Brooke get dressed, and making sure she was wearing a garter belt for the groom to remove, she had left. The day had been a dream and it was coming to an end.

Once they arrived at Jameson's house, which was on the other side of the Broward property, the large wooden front door opened before he even touched it and an older woman came out to greet them. She sent Jameson a look. "Mr. and Mrs. Jameson Broward. Welcome."

"Cut it out, Cecelia."

The older woman pressed her hands together. "Do it for me, please."

Jameson sighed then swept Brooke up in his arms.

Brooke released a squeal of alarm. "What are you doing?"

"Trust me. It's easier than arguing with her."

He carried Brooke into the house then set her down. "Happy now?"

"Do it again," Cecelia said. "I want to take a picture."

"That's not going to happen." He went back outside and brought in Brooke's luggage. "Brooke, this is Cecelia O'Dowd, our house manager." The older woman walked up to Brooke and gave her a big warm hug.

"You made such a beautiful bride. I wish I could have stayed for the reception, but I had to make sure everything was ready for you two."

Brooke opened her mouth to thank her, but Cecelia continued before she could.

"I really want you to be comfortable here. Anything you need, you just let me know. I handle all the staff, the chef, the housekeeper and everyone and everything else in between. You don't have to worry about a thing.

Of course, we don't have as big a staff as at the main house, but if you have any trouble with anyone, just let me know."

"It's a pleasure to meet you," Brooke said, stealing glances at the home's interior. She'd never been inside Jameson's house before. It was a modern structure with a brick face and, although it was the middle of the night, she had seen a carefully manicured lawn surrounding it as they drove in. Moonlight spilled through large windows into the living room, where sleek handcrafted teak furniture sat in front of a stone fireplace. Beyond that, Brooke could see into the gourmet-sized kitchen. Why would a single man need a place this big? Did he expect to have a large family of his own one day?

"I'm sure everything is set," Jameson said.

Cecelia nodded. "Of course."

"Good." Jameson waited then Cecelia took the hint and disappeared.

Brooke watched her go. "I like her."

"She's efficient," Jameson said absently. He turned and headed up the stairs with her suitcases and headed down the hall. Brooke followed. Jameson stopped and opened a door. "Your clothes should already be in the master suite." Brooke had made arrangements to have some of her personal items sent by a moving van ahead of the wedding. "I'll be sleeping in the study. Oh, and by the way, I also had a shed converted into your new studio and had most of your equipment transferred there. If there's anything else you need, just let Cecelia know."

"But what will they think?"

"What will who think?"

"Your staff, about us sleeping in separate rooms."

"Cecelia is the only live-in I have, so we shouldn't have any trouble. And I pay the rest of them enough to keep their mouths shut. We have nothing to worry about." He nodded and left.

Brooke entered the bedroom, where a large king-size carved walnut bed stood facing a floor-to-ceiling window, which provided a panoramic view of the farm. A matching set of his and hers drawers sat against each of the walls. Just off to the left of the bed was a handcrafted mirrored table, where she could put on her makeup and jewelry. Brooke knew that it had been added for her benefit. She went to the walk-in closet, which led to a full-size bathroom with a sunken tub and glass-enclosed shower. Brooke went back into the bedroom, and as she began to disrobe, she suddenly felt an overwhelming sense of sadness. This was not how she had dreamed her wedding night would be. She wished Jameson was there with her. She wished he was the one undressing her and enjoying seeing and removing the dark blue silk underwear she was wearing. But wishing was not her reality.

She pushed those thoughts aside. The marriage was a business agreement. That was all. She wiped a tear away and switched her thoughts to hoping Jameson's room was just as comfortable as hers.

She was glad he'd remembered her need for a studio. Earlier in the week he'd told her he'd renovated an old shed on the property, but she was too tired to look at it now, and besides, it was late and she didn't know where it was. She paused when she heard a soft knock. She quickly grabbed a robe then said, "Come in."

"Oh, I almost forgot," Cecelia said. "A package arrived for you, Mrs. Broward. It's over there." She pointed to the corner, where an old battered trunk sat.

"Thank you and please call me Brooke."

"Just so you know, Jameson is one of the easiest men to work for."

"I'm glad," Brooke said, wondering why Cecelia felt the need to mention that.

"So if you have any instructions…" She let her words fade away.

"Oh," Brooke said, finally understanding her request. Cecelia saw her as the new mistress of the house and was probably waiting for Brooke to give her orders. "Sorry, it's been a long day but I'm sure that we'll get to know each other's habits very quickly. Don't change anything right now on my account."

"It's just that the chef always has Mr. Broward's breakfast ready by four in the morning. Would you like your breakfast ready by then also?"

"Seven would be fine and I'm not particular." Although she had grown up on a ranch, Brooke was not one to wake up at the crack of dawn.

Cecelia nodded. "Well, good night then."

Once Cecelia left, Brooke changed into her new nightgown and went over to the trunk. She noticed the address. It was from her college friend Leslie, who had no idea that Brooke's marriage was a sham. Brooke had phoned her and told her about her wedding, but because it had been such short notice, Leslie had been unable to make it. She had promised to send a gift, though. Leslie had excellent taste. The trunk was filled with an assortment of high-priced personal items—four sets of sexy nightdresses with matching nightgowns, silk slippers, a bed cape to take off the chill when needed, a beautiful handmade quilt, two sets of luxurious towels with both of their initials, three sets of silk sheet sets and several sexy lingerie items just for fun.

Brooke picked up one of the filmy nightgowns. Then she heard a slight knock on the door. Before she could reply, Jameson entered the room then stopped. "What's that?" he asked, eyeing the nightgown with interest.

"My friend Leslie sent me a trousseau. She seems to be the only person alive who thinks this marriage is for real." Brooke set the nightgown down.

Jameson nodded, unable to move his gaze from the nightgown. For one brief, wild moment he wanted to be on a honeymoon with Brooke and wanted their wedding night to be real. He wanted Brooke to be waiting in his bed and wearing that nightgown. He'd slept with beautiful women before, so why was she having such an effect on him? It had only been one night. He couldn't feel this way when he had 364 days to go. His marriage suddenly felt like a prison sentence. No wonder it was considered an institution. Kissing her the way he had at the altar had been a mistake, although he didn't regret it; he just hadn't thought he'd enjoy it so much. It had been too long since he'd been with a woman, and now all he could think of was those lips of hers doing a lot more. He'd thought his heart had shut down, but just looking at a little piece of lace had opened up his desires. He noticed her wedding dress laid out on the bed and the somewhat revealing nightgown she was wearing. He averted his eyes.

"We've been married less than a day and I already can't wait until it's over," he said with feeling, gripping the door handle.

When Brooke's gaze fell he silently swore. He'd hurt her, but he hadn't meant to. It wasn't her fault she made him think about things he'd fought hard to forget. He was experiencing feelings he never thought he'd have again. "I'm sorry."

"Don't be," she said in a light tone. "We both know you didn't want this."

Jameson walked across the room over to the trunk. Even though he couldn't offer her a regular honeymoon night, he didn't want her to be unhappy. He picked up the quilt then set it down. "What's this stuff called again?"

"A trousseau."

He frowned. "A true what?"

"A trousseau," Brooke repeated slowly. She started to explain then caught his quick grin. She narrowed her eyes. "You're teasing me."

"Why would I do that? I'm just a big dumb cowboy. I don't know any fancy German—"

"French."

"Words."

Brooke laughed. He had a playful side he rarely showed and she wanted to see more of it. "So you don't know what any of this is for?" she asked, gesturing to the items.

"No, ma'am." He remained standing. He didn't want to get too comfortable.

She pulled out an old-fashioned garter belt and swung it back and forth on her forefinger. "How about this?"

"Not a clue."

She pulled out a couple of pasties with gold tassels. "Or these?"

"No."

Brooke lifted a full-body stocking, with cutouts, and thread her fingers through several of the strategically located holes. "You must have an idea how one could wear this."

Jameson shook his head, his face blank.

"You can't even use your imagination?"

He rested his hands on his hips. "My mind is not that creative."

"I doubt that. I didn't realize you were shy."

"I'm not shy."

"You were shy to dance at the saloon and now you're shy about this."

Jameson folded his arms and his gaze sharpened. "How come this feels like another challenge?"

Brooke fluttered her eyes. "I don't know. I'm just a dumb cowgirl." She lazily walked around him. "I don't know about these things either. I need somebody to teach me."

"I think you already know a lot."

"One never grows too old to learn."

"Are you trying to tell me something?"

"I'm not a kid anymore."

"I know that. And one day you'll have some college-educated yuppie take you away from here." He watched her make another circle around him. "What are you doing?"

"Just walking."

"Are you trying to make me dizzy?"

Yes. "No." Brooke licked her lower lip and slowed her pace. She wanted him to see her as a woman because she'd always seen him as a man. She could flaunt, taunt and tease, but she wanted him to make the first move. "Those college boys aren't really my type."

Jameson rested his hands on his hips but didn't reply.

"It's amazing what nature can teach you. I'm sure like you, your father never had to sit you down and tell you about the birds and the bees." She continued to lazily walk around him. "I remember when I saw my first bull. I should have been scared, but I wasn't. I was in awe. It was so beautiful and big." She stopped at Jameson's side and looked up at him. His eyes were dark and magnetic. "It was big all over. This wild massive beast went for our little heifer with energy I'd never seen before. That's when I became frightened, but soon I saw the heifer wasn't scared," Brooke said, her voice dropping to a whisper and her gaze sweeping over his face as if she were memorizing every detail. "The heifer expected it and the bull didn't hurt her. She could take him no matter how big and powerful he was. Yes, I learned a lot that day. What do you think?"

For the first time in his life Jameson didn't feel like thinking at all. He grabbed her and kissed her. He hadn't planned to. It was an impulsive decision and completely unlike him, but he did it anyway. He meant to make it quick, playful, but the moment his lips touched hers everything changed. He felt as if the ground had shifted under him.

Jameson pulled away and stared at her shocked expression. The air seemed to still, filled with an electric sense of anticipation and the sound of their breathing. He shook his head, as if to wake himself from a trance, dropped his hands to his side and promptly left the room.

He stumbled to his study and sat down at his desk. What had just happened? He rested a hand against his heart. It was racing, and that wasn't like him. But, no, that was wrong. He had been like this once before, with someone else. He couldn't let himself fall for another Palmer. What was it about those women that seemed to be his weakness? It wasn't because she was beautiful; he was used to that. Then what was it? Loneliness? No. He had all that he needed. Lust? Yes. Definitely. He wanted her.

He wanted to see her mane of curls spread out on a pillow and watch pleasure fill her eyes. He ran a hand down his face and took a deep, steadying breath. No, that was all wrong. The marriage was a business proposition. Strictly business. He had to be the rational one. She was basically a kid. Ten years ago she was still in high school. In a year, she'd get her homestead and marry a man that suited her. And that man wasn't him.

Unlike the princesses in a fairy tale, the kiss didn't wake Brooke up; instead it seemed to cast her under a spell. His spell. Once Jameson left, she felt as if she were living in a dream. Her dream of being his bride had come true. That night she slept with a joy in her heart she never thought possible and woke up the next day with an energy that surprised her. She ate a quick breakfast, knowing that if Jameson had been up at four, he would be halfway through his chores by now. However, she hardly saw him that day or the next two days. She busied herself with getting to know Cecelia and the names of the other staff. She wasn't ready to get back to working with her pottery yet, hoping to at least first share a meal with Jameson. With all that had been going on she hadn't even looked at her studio. But after three days of not seeing him, she knew that the connection she'd hoped they'd made that first night was over.

She'd ended up saving her inheritance and breaking her heart.

Chapter 6

Jameson walked into his bedroom weak with exhaustion. It had been a long day. A neighboring cow had gotten lost and had died from eating one of the larkspurs they'd been spraying. The weed seemed extra virulent this year. But work had been his savior and had helped to keep his mind off his new bride. Since that first night, he'd been successful in keeping his distance from her and planned on keeping it that way until winter, when work slowed, then he planned to work more in his office. Jameson tore off his shirt and made his way to the bed without turning on the lights, comforted by the sweet scent in the air. He flopped on the bed, nearly half-asleep, but jerked back up when he fell on a soft form that screamed. He tumbled out of bed and fell to the floor with a thud just as light flooded the room. He turned on his back and stared up at Brooke, who peered down at him from the edge of the bed.

"What are you doing?" she demanded.

He squinted, his eyes not yet adjusted to the light. What was Brooke doing in his bed? He glanced around the room and his gaze fell on the worn trunk—her trousseau. He squeezed his eyes shut and swore. He was in the wrong room.

"I'm sorry. I forgot," he said as he scrambled to his feet. He grabbed his jeans and put them on, glad he hadn't gone any further than removing his shirt and pants. He cleared his throat. "Are you okay? Did I hurt you?"

"No, I'm fine. You just scared me."

Jameson looked around the room once more, wondering where he'd tossed his shirt. "It won't happen again."

"You didn't have to give me your room, you know. I don't mind staying in the study—"

Jameson shook his head, frowning. His shirt was nowhere in sight. "It's my fault I came in here. I should have remembered."

"Or I could fix up one of the extra empty bedrooms."

"Don't worry yourself. This won't happen again."

"You already said that."

"I'm saying it again because I don't want you to worry."

"I'm not worried."

Just then Cecelia came into the room holding a shotgun. "Are you two all right?"

"Put that thing away," Jameson said.

"But I heard a scream. Was it a burglar? Did you chase him away?"

"It's okay now," he said.

"I'm sorry we woke you," Brooke said.

Cecelia looked at them, then began to grin. "Oh, I forgot that you're newlyweds. I'm glad you're okay." She left.

Jameson sighed. "She probably thinks we're playing some sex game. Maybe I should tell her—"

"Oh, no, please don't. I don't want her to feel sorry for me."

"Why would she feel sorry for you?"

Because she thinks you love me, Brooke wanted to say but didn't. "Let it just be between us."

"She's going to have that silly grin on her face tomorrow."

"I don't mind."

He shrugged. "Fine, as long as it doesn't bother you."

"It doesn't. Does it bother you?"

"Ah…there it is." Jameson grabbed his shirt from under the side table and pulled it on. "How it got there I don't know."

"Jameson?"

"Yes?"

"Does it bother you what she thinks about us?"

"Why would it bother me?" He opened the door. "Good night."

"'Night."

Brooke watched him leave. She wished she hadn't screamed, but he really had scared her when he'd fallen on top of her. If he'd asked, she would have invited him to stay. He really did look exhausted and she wanted to be there for him. She wanted to talk to him, to flirt with him, to sleep with him. But he'd made it very clear he wanted nothing to do with her.

When Jameson saw Cecelia early the next day before he headed out the door, he held up a bill between his middle and forefinger. "I'll pay you fifty dollars to forget about last night and an extra five if you'll wipe that expression off your face."

"I'm happy for you." She snatched the bill and tucked it in her back pocket. "But you can keep the five. I can't stop smiling. I knew it was real."

"What?"

"You know I don't listen to gossip, but some people still think your marriage wasn't a love match. Now I know different. Is she still reeling after the death of her father?"

"Yes, and that's why she needs space and to be left alone."

"Poor thing must struggle with feeling guilty about being happy after suffering such a personal loss."

"I'm glad you understand."

"You'll never hear me say a word." She turned. "I only told a couple of people."

He jumped in front of her. "What?"

"I couldn't help myself," she said, looking sheepish. She started to giggle. "If you could have seen your face."

Jameson didn't smile. He folded his arms and waited.

Cecelia stopped giggling and sighed. "I didn't say too much."

"Who did you talk to?"

"I may have mentioned it to the chef and Frank."

Jameson held out his hand. "Give me the fifty back."

She reluctantly placed it in his palm. "It was funny, though."

"Not to me."

Unfortunately, his ranch hands thought it was hilarious and teased him throughout the day as they worked on checking and cleaning some of the machinery.

"Hey, heard you had a wild night," Frank said.

"Obviously you weren't as tired as the rest of us," another said.

"Hey, if I had a woman like that, I wouldn't be tired either."

"So, what made her scream?" Frank asked.

"Maybe it was her first time and she'd never seen a man before?"

They laughed.

"All right, all right, that's enough," Jameson said.

"No, really. What did you do to make her scream?" Frank asked.

"None of your business," he said in a tone that let them know the topic was closed.

Brooke was mortified with what Cecelia would think. "I'm truly sorry about last night," she said.

Cecelia waved her hand, dismissing her apology. "You don't have to say a thing. It's your house, and you can do what you want. I really want you to feel comfortable here. I know moving takes a lot of adjustments. I guess what I'm trying to say is that we're not here to judge you. We're here to help you."

"Thank you." But in truth Brooke didn't feel like she belonged there. Jameson didn't need her to run the house or the ranch. Everywhere she looked she could see how much he didn't need a wife. There would be no dinner parties to host or children to raise. He was fine on his own. She felt like an extra appendage.

So she decided she should look after herself. She was now ready to focus on her art again and her upcoming show. At least in her studio she wouldn't feel useless. She had hoped to convince Jameson to take the day off and go with her, but she hadn't been able to find him. It was going to be the first time visiting her new studio and she was excited.

Brooke drove over to the shed where he'd made her studio. She opened the door, and what she saw left her speechless. He had told her he'd cleared a shed for her to use, but she hadn't expected an architectural marvel. Jameson had installed several different kilns, an up-to-date pottery kick wheel, a small style clay maker, several porcelain ball mill jars for storing her different glazes, a portable spray booth and a large working table with an assortment of pottery tools.

The layout of the studio allowed easy movement from one part of the studio to the other. The open design had drop panels from the ceiling to concentrate the kiln's fumes and heat, which could be exhausted from the studio. The area where she would throw, model and decorate her finished pieces was spacious and well lit.

Ware racks were everywhere, displaying both items she had finished and those she was working on. She also saw an enclosed glass case, where she could store some of her finished pieces for viewing.

Overwhelmed with emotion, Brooke backed out and closed the door.

Chapter 7

Jameson was returning from the stables when he saw Brooke outside the shed. She was sitting on the ground with her knees drawn up to her chest and her head down. He raced over to her, the sound of her crying growing louder the closer he got. He became alert and looked around to see what could be the cause of her distress.

"What's wrong?" he asked once he reached her. "What happened?"

Brooke glanced up at him. Her eyes and nose red. She opened her mouth then started to cry again.

Jameson stood above her, feeling helpless. "Are you hurt?"

She shook her head.

"Did you get bad news?"

She shook her head again.

He sighed, then kneeled down in front of her. "What's wrong?" he asked gently.

"It's the shed. I didn't even think you were listening when I asked for a place to work."

"Of course I was listening." He bit his lip. Maybe he hadn't been listening enough. He'd had his mother organize the wedding, but he'd taken charge of renovating the shed. Perhaps he'd gotten something wrong. "You don't like it?"

"It's so beautiful," she said in a choked voice. "Nobody in Granger has ever respected me as an artist like you have."

"But I didn't do anything."

Brooke looked at him with a shocked expression. "You didn't do anything?" She jumped to her feet then darted inside and pointed to the shelves. "You have my work displayed like they are museum pieces." She pointed to the kiln. "You installed a kiln that's top of the line. You paid attention to every detail."

As Jameson followed her in he felt his face redden, embarrassed by her praise. "Well, I just know how important it is to have the right tools," he said. He remembered first being annoyed by the prospect of moving all her work to the shed. He'd gone to her house to see what she had in her makeshift workshop so that he could tell the workers what needed to be done, and when he had seen some of her work he had immediately been impressed. He remembered the pictures she used to draw as a child, but what he'd seen was the work of an accomplished artist. She created pottery with Western designs on them that celebrated ranch life. He'd heard about her work but had never seen them in person. Her pieces showed love for the ranch life that he felt but could never express.

"Thank you so much," she said.

Jameson shoved his hands in his pockets, both embarrassed and pleased by her gratitude. "It's nothing. I'm just surprised you're not better known."

Brooke smiled. "I'm not too known in Granger, but I've had shows all over the state. Actually, I have a show coming up in a week that I'm preparing for."

"I'm glad. You're really good. I could never do something like this."

"Would you like to try?"

He paused. "Try what?"

She pointed to a pottery wheel. "This. Let me show you." When she saw him glance toward the door, she grabbed an apron and said, "It won't take long." She draped the apron over his head then tied it in the back.

"I told you, I'm not creative."

"And I plan to prove you wrong."

Brooke showed Jameson how to throw the clay and then helped him form the ball into a bowl shape. He had the perfect hands for it—solid and capable—and the clay seemed to respond to his touch. Usually new potters had no control and let the clay become misshapen, but somehow he was a natural and able to keep all the sides even and smooth.

"I don't know what I'm doing."

"Whatever you're doing, it's working."

"I can see why you like this. It's relaxing," Jameson

said, enjoying the feel of the wet clay beneath his hands. He imagined the clay being her body. As he molded, pushed and formed the shapeless piece of clay he could feel his manhood become hard…. "I'm done now," he said abruptly.

"Okay, let me show you how to take it off the wheel and put it in the kiln."

Jameson went over to the sink and washed his hands. "You can do it for me."

"But—"

He quickly dried his hands and took off the apron. "I won't bother you anymore. I'm glad you like the space." He had to get a hold of himself. Jameson walked out the door and marched away from Brooke's studio as fast as his legs could take him without running.

Brooke watched him go. He was even more wonderful than the man she'd thought him to be. She remembered when she'd first fallen for him. She'd been crying then, too, but for a different reason. Her beloved dog Radar had died. Neither her father nor sister could understand her sorrow. Radar had lived a long life and he had been a working dog, not a pet. And the death of an animal was normal for a rancher, but Radar's death had struck her hard. They'd had a bond no one else could understand. She sat on the back patio with Radar's collar, unable to stop the stream of tears.

"Still crying over that silly dog?" Meredith had said, coming to the patio with a pitcher of lemonade. "Sometimes you act like you're five instead of fifteen. Don't you think so, Jameson?"

Brooke quickly wiped her tears, horrified that he would see her blubbering like a baby. She didn't want him to make fun of her, too.

But he hadn't. Instead he had handed her a tissue and sat down beside her. "There's nothing wrong with crying when you're sad." He glanced down at the collar she held. "Radar was a good friend of yours?"

Brooke sniffed and nodded, basking in the compassion in his brown eyes.

"He was a dog!" Meredith said, clearly exasperated.

Jameson ignored her. "Meredith doesn't understand animals the way we do."

Before Meredith could argue, the phone had rung and she went inside to answer it.

Jameson then had lightly patted Brooke on the shoulder. "You'll be okay."

Brooke blinked back a fresh wave of tears. His tenderness had made her heart ache more. "Radar is one of the last memories I have of my mother. She'd bought him as a puppy and let me go with her to choose him. I remember her training him and—" Brooke stopped, unable to finished.

"Now that he's gone you feel you've lost your mother all over again?"

She'd nodded, relieved that he understood and hadn't make her feel childish.

"But you can't lose what you've never lost. Your mother is always with you. In your heart and in the memories you keep."

Brooke thought of his words now as she watched Jameson walk away. He was in her heart and she had memories of him, but she wondered what she could do to make more with him.

The next day, as evening colored the sky in purple and red hues, Brooke walked around the ranch with her sketchbook in hand. She'd been married to Jameson for two weeks, but she'd rarely seen him. He was a hard man to pin down. If he wasn't working on the ranch, he was in his office looking over paperwork or in town on business. After numerous attempts to try to eat a meal with him, she'd given up and accepted that they were meant to live separate lives, although she still thought of the time she'd managed to get him to stay with her in her pottery studio. Fortunately, she had the land to keep her busy sketching. It offered so many magnificent views to choose from—the cabins in the distance, the mountains and trees, but she headed for the stables instead. She loved drawing horses. She stepped inside and saw Jameson with an emaciated-looking horse as a black dog lay nearby. She slowly approached them.

"That can't be one of your horses."

"He is now."

"Where did you get him?"

"Found him."

Brooke shook her head. "You don't just 'find' a horse."

"I did."

She sighed, irritated. "Please don't lie to me."

"I'm not. I did find him, and another one, at one of those traveling carnivals. He was tied to a post and looking miserable. Poor Royal Thunder was being ridden into the ground."

Brooke's eyes widened. "So you stole him?"

Jameson didn't meet her gaze. "I know he looks bad now, but he's getting the very best care. He's already seen the vet and furrier. The dentist will come by tomorrow. He's not eating as much as he should and that could be because his teeth hurt."

"Jameson, did you steal?"

He turned to her and rested a hand on his chest. "Do I look like the kind of man who'd steal a horse?"

"No, and that's probably why you'd get away with it."

"It would be difficult to steal a horse from a carnival. Let alone two."

"You're clever enough to do it."

He flashed a lazy smile. "Do you want to hand me over to the sheriff?"

"You can't do things like that. It's dangerous."

"I couldn't leave them there." He laughed at her expression. "Don't worry—I didn't steal them. I left some money and *then* I took them because our local horse rescue didn't have any space."

"What do you mean you 'left some money'?"

"They were going to be seized anyway. I made it worth his while."

"What if the owner changes his mind and comes looking for them?"

His grin turned devious. "It's a big county. Where would he start?"

"I'm married to a horse thief."

"Rescuer. Like I said, I compensated the owner, although he didn't deserve it." He looked at the horse and tenderly stroked it. "Don't miss me too much."

"Why would I miss you?"

"I was talking to the horse."

"Why would she miss you then?"

"I'll be gone for two days on business."

Why couldn't the man stay put? If he wasn't racing out of her studio or working, he was disappearing for days. She didn't need to know the specifics. Plenty of things could take a man out of town. Brooke wasn't naive—she knew that was the life of a rancher and because their marriage was a farce, she couldn't expect better. At least she now knew what to expect. She had to lead her own life. Besides, she had a show in a couple of days and she'd be traveling out of town also. He never asked about her work, or private life, so she didn't tell him.

Brooke didn't see Jameson off the next morning. Instead she spent time in her studio trying not to think about him. She was putting glaze on one of her pieces when her cell phone rang.

"Hello?"

"I don't mean to bother you," Cecelia said. "But since Jameson's away..."

"What's wrong?"

"I just went into the stables and Royal Thunder... is down."

"I'll be right there." Brooke washed her hands, put her supplies away and then hurried over to the stable, afraid of what she would find. The horse looked bad.

In addition to Cecelia, one of the stable hands, a youthful-looking young man, was standing over the horse with a grim expression. "She's been down for a while, and we've got to get her up." Brooke knew the importance of getting Royal Thunder up and walking. His internal organs would be crushed by his size if he stayed down too long.

"I've called the vet, but she's on the other side of town taking care of sick cows."

"We don't have much time. Where's the equipment to lift him?" Brooke asked, rolling up her sleeves.

"Over there," the stable hand said.

"Set it up while I get more hands." Brooke knew horses but not well enough to know all that needed to be considered. She needed the advice of experts.

She pulled out her cell phone and telephoned the main house, relieved when Gwendolyn answered. "I could really use your help and Laney's, too."

The two women were at Brooke's side within minutes and looked at the horse in horror. "Where did it come from?" Laney asked.

"Jameson found it wandering," Brooke said.

"But he's not wild," Laney said.

"That doesn't matter right now," Gwendolyn said, taking charge. "We need to get him up." They strapped the horse into the electric harness, then lifted it.

For the rest of that day and all night the women alternated every three hours walking Royal Thunder around the stable and giving him fluids. If he survived the night, they had a fighting chance. When dawn came, the horse was still walking. "The vet will be here later," Gwendolyn said as she hung up her cell phone. "I think the biggest crisis is over. But I suggest we watch him for one more night. I have a dinner party with important guests tonight, but I'll give you some instructions on what to do before the vet arrives."

Cecelia was reading one of her favorite novels when she heard a car horn honking nonstop. It was rare to hear that, but she thought that perhaps kids were joyriding somewhere. She soon smelled something burning. She checked the kitchen but couldn't find anything that could be the cause. She went back to reading, but the smell wouldn't go away and neither did the honking horn. It sounded really close. She walked to the kitchen, then went out into the garage and a cloud of smoke enveloped her. When it dissipated she saw that her Jeep was on fire. She grabbed a bucket, ran back into the house and filled it with water from the kitchen sink.

Brooke came into the kitchen. "What's that smell?"

"My Jeep. Don't worry—I'll take care of it." She hurried outside.

Brooke raced after her, then halted when she saw the sight. "Wait, don't!" she said, but her warning came too late. Cecelia threw the water on the fire and it reacted like gasoline, becoming like a bomb explosion. Cecelia fell to the ground with the back of her arms scorched.

"Get inside," Brooke ordered. She looked around and saw some old wool blankets. She grabbed them and doused the flames. In seconds the crisis was over. She raced back inside to look at Cecelia. "Let me take you to the hospital."

"What just happened?" Cecelia asked in a daze.

"You threw water on an electrical fire. It's danger-ous to do that because electricity acts like a conductor."

"I'm so stupid. But I don't want to trouble you." She winced as she began to feel the pain from her burns.

"It's no trouble."

Brooke drove Cecelia to the hospital, where she got her wounds cleaned and bound. Brooke's swift action had prevented her from suffering anything worse than first-degree burns. She wouldn't be able to use her left hand for several weeks, though. "But I have work to do," Cecelia argued on the ride home. "I have a house to run."

"Let me call Jameson."

"Oh, no, please don't. He's got enough on his mind. My job is to make his life easy and I want to keep it that way. I just have so much to do. I have a plumber coming tomorrow and—"

Brooke knew that Cecelia wouldn't be able to do everything on her own. She'd planned to leave for her show the next day, but she knew she would have to can-cel. "Just tell me what needs to be done and I'll help."

Brooke held the phone away from her ear while her broker, Matthew Rainey, shouted at her for canceling her appearance at the Sugarloaf Craft Festival in Helena. He handled all of her sales transactions and worked with the various galleries she had contracts with. Brooke sold her work under another name. She had been a pro-tégé in high school and began making and selling her work at county fairs from age sixteen. Creating and sell-ing her pottery meant a lot to her, but right now Royal

Thunder and Cecelia meant more, and she knew she couldn't leave at such a crucial time. Once Matthew took a breath she said, "I'm sorry, but I can't make it. There's been an emergency here at the ranch."

"I don't care if the damn place is falling down. You can't cancel. You have a lot riding on this show."

"There will be other shows."

"You're going to lose *a lot of money.* Also, I won't get my commission and there are buyers anxiously waiting to see and purchase your work."

"I can't make it."

"Let me talk to your husband."

"He's not here."

"He's left you already?"

"He's away on business."

"Are you really that naive?"

Matthew usually had his head in the gutter, but he was good at his job. "Don't be a jerk. He's not cheating on me."

"He'd be stupid if he did, but they're not too bright out there, are they? They wear big hats to make up for little brains."

"You're pissing me off on purpose."

"It's what I do, honey. I want you to really think about what you're doing and why."

"I know why."

He swore. "I knew I shouldn't have let you get married."

Brooke's voice rose in surprise. "Let me?"

"When you sent me that note about getting married, I almost wept. You're only twenty-five. You could have waited another two years. By then, your career would have been more established. But things are already falling apart. You've been married less than two weeks and he's started ruining your career."

"He's not ruining anything. This is my decision. I pay you to take care of my business. That's all I'm asking you to do."

"Well, honey, it's your choices that stink. If you weren't so beautiful, I'd have walked away. After your father died, I thought you'd finally move out of that hick town."

"This is my home. I'm my most creative here. Georgia O'Keefe had New Mexico, and I have Montana. Besides, I'm talented as well as beautiful."

"Yeah," he said as an aside. "That, too. Fine. I'll see what I can do."

"Thanks, Matthew. You know I'll make it up to you," Brooke said, then hung up. Her mood quickly dimmed. She hated when Matthew only mentioned her looks, as if that—and not her talent—was her biggest selling point. Sometimes she wondered if he really thought she had any. In town her art was treated like a hobby; it was only outside of Granger where she'd started seeing true success. Matthew had been the first to talk about her art as a career, so she was grateful for that. But even then, she'd still gotten more comments about her looks than her work from both him and interested buyers. That's why Jameson's response to her art had touched her. He was sincere. He didn't flatter her. He treated her like an equal and respected her passion, which made it easy for her to respect him.

Now her only hope was that Royal Thunder would make it so that he would see his new master again, and that Cecelia would be okay. And she couldn't wait to see him, too.

Chapter 8

As a child, Jameson had rarely gotten into trouble, leaving most juvenile antics to his younger siblings, Wes and Laney. But when he did do something wrong, he was always ready for the consequences. This time he wasn't prepared for the sight of his mother coming at him like an angry mare as he parked his truck.

"Where did you get that horse?"

He froze. "What horse?"

"Don't play dumb with me."

"I honestly don't know what you're talking about."

She pointed to his stables. "I'm talking about that poor horse that Brooke had to spend two full days and nights nursing back to health. Oh, don't worry, he's fine now, but I haven't seen a horse look that bad in years. Now, where did you get him?"

"It's a long story. You're sure he's all right?" He waved his hands when his mother bristled with outrage. "I'm sorry I asked. I trust your judgment."

"Then I demand you tell me what's going on. Why do you have a horse like that?"

"I found him."

"Where?"

"Like I said, it's a long story."

She sighed. "You're not going to tell me, are you?"

He only smiled.

"Stubborn as a mule and as tough as a horseshoe." She wagged her finger at him. "You're lucky Brooke was here. Especially with poor Cecelia."

He paused. "What about Cecelia?"

"Oh, I guess they didn't want to worry you about that."

"Worry me about what?"

"I'm sure Brooke will explain everything. She's been managing the place well."

"I was just gone two days. What could have happened?"

"Talk to Brooke. I hope you thank her properly."

Jameson folded his arms. "Properly, huh? Are you offering up any ideas?"

"Roses. Hand-delivered by you."

Jameson shook his head and turned to his house. "Sorry, that's not my style, but I'll think of something."

"Try to be romantic. I don't want you to lose…" Her words fell away.

He slowly turned. "Go on. You don't want me to

lose what? Another woman? Do you think I drove Meredith away?"

"I didn't mean that," Gwendolyn said, looking chagrined.

"Has Brooke talked about leaving?" Jameson asked, suddenly angry. "If she wants to leave, that's her choice. I'm not holding her prisoner."

"Brooke didn't mention anything about leaving. I just…a woman needs to know she matters. That she's valuable to you. I just think you should show it somehow. You've lived on your own for so long, I don't know if you realize what sharing a life with someone else means."

Jameson sighed, letting his anger die away. He knew his mother was only trying to help. She didn't know how raw his wounds still were. "I'll send her flowers."

"Give them to her."

"You think that will make a difference?"

She started to smile. "Do it and you'll see."

Jameson went to see Cecelia first. She sat in the living room with her arms bandaged. He sat down in front of her. "What happened?"

"I've got scars to match my hair now," she said with a bright grin.

He didn't return the expression. "Are you okay?"

"I'm fine now, thanks to Brooke."

"What happened?" he repeated, this time with more force.

"I tried to put out an electrical fire in my Jeep with water, and I got burned. Afterward I noticed a letter on my desk that I had not gotten around to opening. It seems that model has been recalled for that reason. Don't worry—we got it towed away."

"Are you sure you're okay?"

"I'm fine. Brooke's been helping me manage the house. And she's been taking good care of Royal Thunder."

He swore. "I bet she hasn't been pleased with that."

"She hasn't complained. She took over and let me rest. She's been acting just the way a wife should. She makes me want to heal up fast or I'll be out of a job."

"Never," Jameson said with feeling. "You'll always have a place here."

"You're too good to me."

He stood. "Just let me know if you need anything.

"I will. By the way, when you thank her make sure the roses are red."

Jameson rolled his eyes. "Have you been talking to my mother?"

"No, but flowers are always nice."

"I gave a woman flowers once. She preferred jewelry. She said it lasted longer."

"And I bet you that girl's heart was as cold as those jewels."

Jameson shrugged. He was in no mood to talk about it. Cecelia hadn't known Meredith but had likely heard the story about his breakup. "I'll see what I can do."

"Brooke isn't like that other woman. Trust me."

Brooke lay on her bed thinking about her phone call with Matthew and the canceled pottery show. Sometimes he reminded her too much of Meredith. She and her sister weren't close and Meredith only found reasons to criticize her. Over the past ten years they'd rarely spoken, and the last time she'd seen her sister was at their father's funeral. But she was never shy to voice her opinion, and Brooke could just imagine her berating her now for not going to the craft show. Her sister wouldn't understand the choice she'd made. She remembered an old phone call with her years ago.

"There's nothing in Granger for you except Dad," she'd said. "No museums, live theater, fine dining, posh hotels. The closest I ever want to be to a ranch again is the Broadway production of *Oklahoma!* That's why I couldn't marry Jameson. I had to leave. The ranch will take up your life. It took up Dad's life, and Jameson's no different. If you won't listen to me about anything else, listen to this. Don't marry a cowboy. You'll waste away from neglect. A ranch is a selfish mistress."

Those words still echoed in Brooke's mind that evening. She knew she couldn't fight the seductive nature of the Montana prairie. And Jameson would be home soon, but they'd just keep passing each other, as strangers. She didn't know how she'd be able to hold up the charade for another eleven months. Brooke turned her head toward the door at the sound of a knock. It was probably Cecelia. She always provided a bright spot in her day. Brooke rested her arms behind her head. "Come in."

"Were you sleeping?" a deep voice said.

Brooke sat up and stared at Jameson. "You're back?" She scrambled off the bed and stood, pressing her hair down. Why did he have to choose now to talk to her? She must look a mess. Her gaze fell to the dozen red roses in his hand. "What are you doing?"

He held out the roses. "These are for you. My mother told me what you did and how you saved Royal Thunder's life, and Cecelia can't stop singing your praises."

"Oh."

"What you did really means a lot to me."

She nodded. "I see."

When she made no move to take the bouquet, he frowned. "You don't like roses?"

"No, it's just that you didn't have to go through all this trouble."

"What would you have preferred?" he said in a tense voice. "Let me guess, a diamond bracelet or maybe something to wear."

"No. A simple hug would have been nice."

He blinked. "A hug?"

"Yes, as you would a friend. Our marriage may be false, but I still like to consider you as a friend."

"I don't have many friends."

Brooke bit her lower lip, knowing the risk she was taking, but she was determined not to back down. He may not see her as a wife, but she wanted, at least, some kind of a relationship with him that didn't make them strangers. "You have me."

Jameson set the flowers aside then pulled Brooke into his embrace. "Is this what you had in mind?" he whispered into her ear.

Brooke briefly shut her eyes, pressed her cheek against his chest and held him close. "Yes." She drew away and looked up at him. She opened her mouth to say more, but he smothered her words with a kiss.

Unlike the kiss at the ceremony, she knew this one was meant only for her, and that made it sweeter than she could have imagined. For a moment it made her thoughts spin, and she imagined him wanting her as much as she wanted him. She wrapped her arms around his neck and deepened the kiss. Jameson moaned with satisfaction. His hand dipped to her blouse. "Are you wearing anything from your trousseau underneath this?"

"No, but I can—"

"We'll save them for another time," he said, removing her blouse.

Jameson carried her over to the bed. Brooke reached for his shirt but couldn't undo the buttons. "Nervous?" he asked.

"A little," she admitted, annoyed that her hands wouldn't stop shaking.

"Relax. We're friends, remember?"

Brooke forced a smile. He saw her as a friend, but he was the love of her life and she had more to lose if the night was a disaster. She'd been flirting with him for weeks and she had to deliver.

"This is going to be good," Jameson said, as if reading her thoughts, his dark eyes filled with a sensuous promise. Brooke felt all her fears immediately melt away as he removed her clothes with exquisite care. "I wanted to do this the first night."

Brooke slid her hand under his shirt. "I wish you had."

Jameson kissed her between her breasts. "I'll make up for lost time."

She tugged on the front of his shirt.

He glanced down at her, confused. "What are you doing?"

"I still can't get your damn buttons undone. What do you use, Super Glue?"

Jameson laughed and quickly undid them himself, then tossed the shirt on the ground.

Brooke splayed her hands over his chest. "From now on I want you to only wear T-shirts."

"We'll discuss that another time. Right now, let's focus on the birds and the bees."

Her hand slid to the center of him. "Or bulls and—"

His mouth covered hers. She melted into his hot flesh, which was more intoxicating than any wine she'd ever tasted. Her hands moved over his as if he were a new batch of clay. But she didn't need to mold him into anything—he was a study in perfection. She'd given her heart to him many times, but that night she wanted his, so she surrendered her body to him.

And Jameson took it with a hunger he didn't even know he had. He couldn't get enough of her. He sank between her soft thighs and used his tongue to taste her. And then they both rode a tide of passion until they fell listless on the bed, still entangled.

"To think I only came in to give you flowers," Jameson said, his voice muffled against the pillow.

Brooke giggled. "I'm glad you did. I'll never look at roses the same way again."

Jameson turned on his side and lifted himself up on his elbow. "Besides saving Royal Thunder's life and taking care of Cecelia and the house, what else have you been up to while I was away?"

"I was preparing for the pottery fair."

"So when is your show?" Jameson asked.

"Gone."

"Gone?"

"I canceled."

"Why? Wait. Damn, I'm sorry," Jameson said as he realized the date had passed.

"Don't be. I had to. I wanted to. I would have felt awful if I'd left. There will be other shows," Brooke said, then kissed him and they soon forgot about anything else.

The next night was the same and Brooke felt like everything was perfect until an unexpected guest came to visit.

Chapter 9

"There's someone here to see you," Cecelia said.

"Me?" Brooke asked, taking off her work apron and wiping her hands. She'd been working in her studio when Cecelia called her cell phone. "I wasn't expecting anyone."

"She's at the house. I didn't think you'd want to be disturbed in your studio."

"Thank you. I'll be right there."

Brooke returned to the house wondering who would have come for a surprise visit. It couldn't be Meredith; Cecelia would have said so. Mitch would have called her if there was something wrong, and he usually handled everything himself. Also, Cecelia said "she." Brooke continued to guess as she walked inside the house. She halted when she saw who sat in the living room. The young woman looked up and saw Brooke, then rushed over to her and gave her a fierce hug.

Just as she had in college, her friend Leslie blew into Brooke's life like a mini whirlwind. She was small and compact with the energy of a New Yorker on a caffeine high, and she talked as if every moment might be her last. She lived in Colorado but traveled extensively.

"Hi, I just had to see you. I was so annoyed that I missed your wedding, but it happened so fast I wasn't able to make it—"

"Yes, I know—"

"But I thought I'd be able to at least see you at the craft festival, but you weren't there so I thought I'd come out and see how you were doing. Oh, my God, this place is amazing. When you told me you came from a small town I wasn't expecting this. Did you marry into Montana royalty or something? Do you have pictures from the wedding? Where is he?" She peered behind Brooke. "No, wait, I think I see him."

Brooke turned and saw Jameson coming down the hall.

"Is it?" Leslie asked.

"Yes."

Leslie gave a low whistle. "Rich and sexy. Did you like the trousseau?"

"I told you I did."

"I was talking to him," Leslie said, holding her hand out to Jameson, who'd come up behind Brooke. "Leslie Mifflin." She sat back down. Jameson and Brooke sat across from her on the love seat.

Jameson shook her hand. "A pleasure to meet you."

"Don't worry—I won't be staying long. I only plan to spend a night, then I have somewhere else I need to be. I just wanted to stop by and see how my friend was doing." She turned to Brooke. "Why didn't you make the festival? I remember you telling me how excited you were about exhibiting there. You'd been talking about it for months. I was stunned when I didn't see you."

"An emergency came up."

"I really didn't expect this for you," she said, admiring the house and the scenery outside. "In college all you talked about was how you wanted to get away from your father's ranch and live like an artist."

Brooke glanced at Jameson. "That was a long time ago."

"Not that long. Remember how much fun we had going to the museums and listening to the symphony? I'd never thought you'd end up marrying a cowboy, but I realize love makes you do crazy things."

"I like Granger."

"That's a new tune. I never thought you'd come back here after what you'd said about feeling stuck."

Brooke remembered that she had complained once, when she'd erroneously thought Jameson had started seriously dating another woman—only to discover it was just another date from the cowboy auction he entered every year. She'd wanted to make herself forget about him, and the town, and she'd said things to help her get over him. It hadn't worked, but unfortunately Leslie had remembered that particular conversation.

"It had been a hard time in my life. I don't feel that

way anymore. I don't think I ever really did—it was just a painful period I was going through."

"You don't have to explain," Jameson said. "Some people enjoy this town more than others."

"Uh-huh," Leslie said, her gaze darting between them. "Did I say something wrong?"

"No," Jameson stood. "I'll let you two ladies catch up."

"Oh, don't leave yet," Leslie said, lightly tugging on his shirt sleeve. "Tell me how it happened."

"How what happened?"

"How you two met."

"I told you that we've known each other a long time," Brooke said.

"Oh, yes, that's right. He's your secret crush. The guy you've loved since you were fifteen."

At that moment, Brooke felt like falling through the floor. She'd forgotten she'd told Leslie that, but she'd added that tidbit of information as part of her story for why she was getting married so suddenly, saying that he was a man she'd always loved and that he'd finally returned her feelings. But Jameson didn't seem affected by Leslie's words.

"So, how did you propose?"

"I took her out riding one day," Jameson said, then elaborated on a story that wasn't true. But her friend fell for it. Brooke was grateful that Jameson was helping her to save face, but she still wished herself far away.

"That is so romantic," Leslie said once Jameson had finished. She jumped up. "Brooke, could you show me where the bathroom is?"

Brooke did, and the moment her friend was out of hearing she turned to Jameson. "What are we going to do?"

"What do you mean? I think we're handling it well."

"She can't see that we're sleeping in separate rooms."

"I'll have Cecelia close the door to the study and I'll spend the night with you." He winked. "I'm getting used to it anyway."

"That won't be enough."

"Why not?"

"It will look strange."

"How will she know? Does she snoop?"

"She's going to want a tour of the house."

"What for?"

"Women like to do things like that," Brooke said, growing impatient. "You have to get some of your things moved back into the master suite so it looks like we're sharing the same room."

Jameson shook his head. "It still doesn't make sense to me, but since appearance and what people think matters to you, I'll tell Cecelia."

Brooke showed Leslie her studio first. She wanted to get her friend out of the house so that Cecelia and Jameson could move his things and cover up any hints that Brooke and Jameson weren't living like happy newlyweds.

"Wow," Leslie said, looking around. "He built this for you?"

"Yes, he converted an old shed."

"You know that cowboys aren't my thing, but if I

find one who likes to spend money like this I would definitely change my mind. So what's going on between you two?"

Brooke folded her arms and feigned a look of confusion. "What do you mean?"

"I mean, you and Jameson don't act like any newlywed couple I've seen. You don't have any pictures of your wedding up anywhere, and you seem embarrassed about me mentioning your childhood crush on him."

"It's because I have never told him before."

"Why not?"

Brooke glanced away, unable to meet her friend's interested stare. "I just never had the chance," she said, trying to sound vague. She lowered her arms then looked at Leslie. "So why are you really here?"

This time it was Leslie's turn to look uncomfortable. "I told you."

"It's not like you to just drop by out of the blue. I'm not saying that I'm not happy to see you, but tell me the truth."

"I heard that Samara Lionne is here."

"She is, so what?"

"Do you know her?"

"No. What would a Hollywood actress and I have in common?"

"Well," Leslie said, drawing out the word. "You're both artistic."

Brooke paused. "Why do you want to know?"

"I've always wanted to be an actress."

Brooke stared at her, stunned. "You never told me that before."

"I've never told anyone, but then I saw that Samara Lionne was in your town and I saw it as a sign. What if I could meet her and get cast in one of her movies? It doesn't have to be a big role. I'd take a walk-on just to get started. Couldn't you just see me in a movie? And I've seen all of hers and I think she's great. We'd work so well together. I see myself in comedy or a drama or both. You know those drama-comedies that independent filmmakers like to make. I'd be the perfect comic relief or the tragic best friend. I—"

"I thought you said you were only spending one night," Brooke cut in before her friend got ahead of herself.

Leslie bit her lip. "Well, if you could get me an interview I could spend a little more time. I'm flexible."

Brooke held up her hand. "No one has said she's doing a picture here."

"But it's a possibility. Why else would she end up in this place?"

"Maybe she wants to get away from people like you."

Leslie grimaced. "You think it's a bad idea?"

"I think it's a terrible idea."

Leslie sighed. "I knew you'd say that." She looked around. "I'm happy for you. This workshop is amazing and so is the house, not to mention your sexy husband, but are you sure this will be enough for you for the rest of your life? Sometimes I envy the Samara Lionnes of this world. I'd love to have a jet-setting, glamorous life instead of just being a curator at a museum few people have ever heard of."

"But you love your job," Brooke said, knowing Leslie's wealthy parents had gotten her the exclusive position. "You love the people you meet and learning the history of the artwork you share with them. I know what I told you in the past, but, yes, I can imagine living the rest of my life here," Brooke said when Leslie opened her mouth. "I'm a changed woman now."

"So, how many kids are you going to have?"

Brooke rolled her eyes. "We just got married and you're already talking about children."

"Have you thought about it?" Leslie pressed.

"So, are you seeing anybody?" Brooke asked, eager to change the subject.

"No, but if Jameson has a brother…"

"He does."

Leslie's eyes lit up.

"But he's taken."

"Damn, just my luck."

They left the studio then walked around the estate. Leslie stopped when she saw a man walking one of the horses. "I know him. He's a top man in the rodeo circuit."

"I didn't know you were interested in the rodeo."

"I'm not, but I once dated a guy who couldn't get enough of it so I pretended to be interested in it for a few months." Leslie looked the man up and down. "Do you think he's taken?"

"I don't know." Brook shook her head. "Oh no, you don't."

"What?"

"You get that look out of your eye. You're leaving tomorrow." When she saw a sly grin spread on Leslie's face, she groaned, knowing her friend intended to stay longer than that. "You're staying no more than two days and I don't want you causing any trouble before that."

Leslie gave Brooke a quick hug. "Thanks." She spread her arms wide and deeply inhaled then eyed the ranch hand again. "There's something about being around nature and all this testosterone that just makes a girl think about sex."

Brooke nudged her. "Try to think about something else."

Leslie laughed then lifted her brows with a look of hope. "Like getting Samara's number?"

"Something besides that."

"Does Jameson know her? A man with his family background has connections."

"Put the idea out of your mind."

"That was quite a story you fed Leslie," Jameson said that night as they prepared for bed.

"Story?"

"Yes, about you loving me since you were fifteen. Very creative."

It's true, she wanted to say but didn't. "Yes, you know me. Always inventive," Brooke said with a hollow laugh.

"What are you going to do with the homestead when you leave?"

"Who said I was leaving?"

"Leslie said you sounded very keen on the idea once."

"That was a long time ago," she said in a tight voice.

"I said I was going through a difficult time." *I didn't want to see you again. I didn't want to see you in love with someone else.*

"And what happens if, or when, a difficult time comes again?"

"Granger is my home. I like to travel, I'll admit that. But I'll always come back here."

"To visit?"

"To stay."

"When the right man comes along, you'll leave and I won't blame you. This kind of life isn't for everyone."

"It's a life that suits me fine. Do you really think I'd be doing this if Granger didn't mean something to me? Do you honestly think I'd marry a man to save my inheritance just for the fun of it? Do you think it's been easy for me to know that you feel roped into this marriage and can't wait for it to end? If there had been another way, you can be sure I would have found it. But I didn't, so here we are counting down the days until we can be free of each other."

"I didn't mean—"

"Do you know why I paint landscapes on my pottery? Because I love the sound of the Montana winds along the prairie and the stillness of a summer night. My roots run just as deep as yours and my love for the land is just as strong. But it's not a betrayal to love other things, too. Like the sound of tinkling glasses in a five-star restaurant in the heart of some cosmopolitan city."

"You're right. You deserve that life."

But I want that life to be with you. Brooke got under the covers.

Jameson sighed. "I'm sorry. I didn't mean to upset you."

"I know. It's just bad enough with my father telling me what to do in his will and then you trying to tell me my own mind."

"It won't happen again."

Brooke started to smile. "You're just nervous because you're afraid I won't have sex with you again."

Jameson raised a brow. "Do I have a right to be nervous?"

"You did, but you made up for it."

"Can I make up for it some more?" He wrapped his arms around her.

"Actually, you already are."

"How?"

"By letting Leslie stay more than one night."

He stepped back. "What do you mean?"

"She just needs a break. She told me she won't stay more than two days, and relax, she has promised me that she won't cause any trouble."

But Leslie did cause trouble. She distracted the ranch hands by walking around wearing a pair of very tight jeans and a halter top. It wasn't summer yet and the weather wasn't warm enough, but Brooke knew the outfit would certainly make the ranch hands hot under the collar. It appeared that Leslie had given up the idea of being introduced to the actress and was now determined to be the star attraction of her own show.

"You need to do something about your friend," Jameson said the next evening after they'd finished dinner and Leslie had disappeared to her room. Brooke and Jameson sat in the living room, both pretending to watch TV.

"What can I do?" Brooke said, feeling helpless.

"Send her home. Now."

"I can't do that. It's only been one day."

"One day too long. If you can't send her home, I can."

"Come on. Just give her one more day."

Jameson shook his head. "Letting one woman into my life was hard enough, let alone two."

Brooke swallowed, feeling guilty about the situation she'd put him in. He was right. He hadn't planned on having to marry her, let alone having to host her friend. But she had to make him understand her position. "Jameson, please try to understand. She's my friend and I care about her."

"I know that and that's why I'm being nice about it. But she's a nuisance. She's flirting with anything on two feet by asking silly questions and laughing at jokes that aren't even funny."

"I think she's lonely."

"I don't care. She's distracting the men and I can't blame them."

"Are you distracted?" Brooke asked with sudden interest.

Jameson grinned. "Brooke, if you leave steak on the table the dogs are going to drool."

"Is that a yes or a no?"

"What do you think?"

"I think you're avoiding the question."

"I'm doing exactly the same as you. So let's both be

honest. Yes, I do notice, but no, she's not my type." He stood. "Now do something about her or I will," he said then left the room.

Brooke covered her face in her hands. She didn't know what she could do without hurting Leslie's feelings. But she didn't want Jameson to be upset. Their relationship was tenuous enough, and she didn't want him thinking she was as silly as Leslie. She felt guilty but trapped at the same time.

"He's right," Cecelia said, coming into the room.

Brooke looked up at her. "You don't like her either?"

"I like her. She's full of life, but she doesn't belong here. She's pretty, but she should know when and where to catch a man's attention. Like at the saloon. Not when he's doing dangerous work."

"I never saw this side of her before." But she had in small doses. In college they'd both enjoyed their new freedom but had never been reckless. Leslie had liked to flirt and had had many boyfriends, but she'd always come to her senses before she did anything stupid.

Brooke went to Leslie's room but was surprised when she knocked and there was no answer. When she opened the door, the room was empty. She searched the house and grounds for her, but couldn't find her anywhere. She called her cell phone but got no reply.

She had to fix this problem before Jameson got more upset. She was about to leave when she heard a strange moaning sound. She walked into the barn, and all the animals looked fine, but the moaning sound continued and grew louder. She followed the sound to one of the stalls and found Leslie tangled up with the ranch hand she'd recognized from the rodeo circuit.

"Did you hear that?" he asked.

"No," Leslie said. "Keep going."

"I could swear I heard something."

"It's probably just one of the animals."

"Or me," Brooke said.

The man swore and scrambled to cover himself. Leslie quickly pulled her skirt down. "I know what you're going to say."

Brooke shook her head. "I don't think you do."

"I'm sorry about this," the ranch hand said.

"You'd better move fast before Frank or Jameson start looking for you."

"You won't say anything?"

"Do your best today and I'll think about it." After he'd gone, Brooke glared at her friend. "I warned you."

"I couldn't help myself."

"You don't even know him." Brooke threw up her hands. "You're not making any sense. First, you want to be an actress, then I find you sleeping with some guy you saw at a rodeo. This isn't like you."

"I know. I lied. I didn't just stop by. I just found out my parents are getting a divorce and I broke up with my boyfriend and I feel awful about myself. I just needed to feel desirable again. I thought this would be a good way to act when other parts of my life are falling apart."

"You're only twenty-five. Plenty of other men are on the horizon. Don't sell yourself short."

"I am short."

"You know what I mean."

"It's easy for you to say. You're beautiful and now rich and you have a man who loves you."

If only that were true. "Life's about a lot more than that."

"Like what?"

"Being happy."

Leslie nodded. "You're right. I'll leave tomorrow. I guess my parents' breakup is hitting me harder than I thought. They'd been married for years and now they can hardly stand each other. It makes me wonder if love ever really lasts."

Brooke wondered the same thing as she prepared for bed that night. Part of her wanted Leslie to stay. She'd enjoyed pretending that she and Jameson shared the same bedroom. She didn't want to go back to the way it had been.

"So?" Jameson asked. He lay against the headboard, his arms folded over his bare chest. "Did you get to talk to her?"

"Yes," Brooke said, pulling on her nightdress then closing the drawer. "She's leaving tomorrow."

"Good. Where was she?"

Brooke froze. "Why?"

He narrowed his eyes. "It's a simple question."

"I don't understand why you're asking it."

"Because I want to know. I'd wanted to talk to you and you were nowhere in the house."

Brooke licked her lip. "We met outside. Leslie had decided to go for a walk. Does it matter?"

"It does when you look guilty."

"You're the one who's suspicious." Brooke got on the bed and straddled his waist, hoping to improve his mood and make him forget about her friend. "Aren't you happy that I've handled this situation?" she asked, inching up her nightgown to expose her thighs.

Jameson lowered his gaze, rested his hand on her leg and slowly trailed a path up until his hand disappeared under her nightie. "She must really have done something. Just tell me, did she break anything?"

"No."

"Then I forgive her," he said, then kissed Brooke, making them both forget Leslie's indiscretion.

As promised, and to Brooke's relief, Leslie left the next morning. For the following few days Jameson and Brooke settled back into their own routine. They both kept themselves busy with their daily chores then spent the nights in each other's arms. And they began experimenting by making love in the afternoons in addition to their nighttime soirees. After one rigorous afternoon interlude, Brooke changed into a pair of jeans and a loose-fitting shirt to go to her workshop then grabbed his cowboy hat. Jameson took it off as she headed for the door. "A woman should know better than to take a man's hat," he said, placing it on his head.

"Oh, come on." She reached for it. "Just for fun."

He moved it out of reach. "It's too big for you anyway."

"I don't care."

"Get your own."

"Don't you know how to share?"

He set the hat firmly on his head. "I'm sharing my bed, but I'm not sharing this."

Brooke made a face. "Not even for a minute?"

"Not even for a second, but you can borrow one of my shirts."

Brooked leaned toward him and lowered her voice. "So, there's nothing I can do to make you change your mind?"

"Nothing."

"Fine." She turned, walked past him, opened one of his dresser drawers, grabbed one of his T-shirts and put it on. She then tied it in the front, leaving her midriff exposed. She walked to the door.

He swore then blocked her path. "I knew your friend was a bad influence. You're not going out like that."

"Why not?"

"Because you look sexy as hell."

She wiggled her hips. "That's the plan. But maybe I should let the ranch hands decide who is more distracting, Leslie or me."

"Do you want their wives coming after you?"

"Not all of them are married." She rested her hands on her hips. "It's either the T-shirt or the hat. You choose."

Jameson rested his arms on the doorframe, effectively blocking her. "Okay, let's come up with a compromise."

"I'm listening."

"You can wear the hat in bed."

"Why would I want to do that?"

Jameson's voice lowered to a seductive rumble. "Ever

ride a mechanical bull before? After tonight I'll give it a whole new meaning."

Brooke untied the shirt. "Then tonight can't come fast enough. If I could make the sun set now, I would."

"And I'd help you." He kissed her and then left the room.

Brooke closed the door to the kiln and thought about what Jameson had planned for the evening. She'd had boyfriends in college, but no man had ever made her feel the way he did. Lately it seemed she really mattered to him. She couldn't believe Meredith had let him go. He was everything she'd imagined him to be and more. He wanted her in bed, he liked her as a friend, but he'd *loved* Meredith. Would he always consider her second best? Would he ever love her? Would he always think of her as Meredith's little sister? They were friends, but would he ever let what they had become something more?

Jameson didn't like what he was hearing, but he made sure that fact didn't show on his face. He sat in the kitchen of the Baileys, where Rod Bailey's wife had ushered them.

"It's a lot of money and we're getting on in years and none of our children want to stay here."

Jameson nodded but he knew that was baloney. Their son was around his age and had talked about raising his family in Granger. But what he noticed most were not the words Mr. Bailey was saying but the look on his face. The Baileys were one of the older families, like the Browards, who had lived in Granger for years. He looked worried, as if he were trying to convince himself about something.

"Who is it?"

"The broker won't say. I did ask, but he said the investor likes to let the money talk for itself."

"And that's it?"

"Yes." It wasn't like Rod Bailey to be so reticent. Even his wife was. They weren't telling him something, but he didn't know what. He didn't want to be suspicious of them. He knew that was how a town got divided. Someone was buying up the town, but he couldn't fight an invisible foe. Whoever the investor or investors were, they were powerful.

Chapter 10

The summons came right on schedule. Jameson looked at Cecelia as he sat behind his desk in his study.

"You said tonight?" Jameson asked, annoyed.

Cecelia nodded. "She said she was afraid if she told you sooner, you'd come up with an excuse not to go."

His mother was right. Dinner at the main house with family wasn't high on his list of priorities. "I already had plans for tonight."

Cecelia looked alarmed. "I'm sorry. I didn't see anything on your calendar."

"Private plans," Jameson corrected.

"Oh," Cecelia said. "Your mother expects you both to dress your best because it will be Brooke's first dinner as a Broward."

Jameson rubbed his chin. "I guess it can't be avoided."

"I think it will be good for Mrs. Broward."

Brooke was just as disappointed as Jameson by their change in plans, but she knew it was an opportunity to stay in the Browards' good graces. "Do you think they'll talk about Samara's upcoming press conference?" she asked as they drove to the main house.

"It's likely. Everyone in town is talking about it. I wonder what Samara's going to say."

"Some locals believe she's going to announce she's filming a movie in town. Others hope she is going to open a movie studio here."

"That's a scary thought."

Dinner that evening consisted of braised asparagus, stuffed mushrooms, oven-roasted potatoes, barbecue pulled pork and rice pilaf. Everything was cooked to perfection, but Brooke could hardly taste a thing. She felt like a fraud. All she could see was how false her relationship with Jameson was compared to the others. Wes and Lydia had postponed going back on vacation and as they sat at the table it was clear how much in love they were. And Gwendolyn and Steven had been in love for years. Grandpa Charles had loved and seemed open to falling in love again. In the glaring light of all this, Brooke knew that all she and Jameson had was a great sex life.

"You've hardly touched a thing," Gwendolyn said, looking at Brooke's plate.

"It's so delicious, I'm trying to savor every bite," Brooke said quickly. "I really enjoy being here with you all."

"Get used to it," Steven said. "We're a family that likes to get together."

"And that's an order," Jameson added.

Gwendolyn shook her head. "Brooke, I don't know what you saw in this surly cowboy."

"He has his own special charm," Brooke said.

"And he also happens to be sitting right here," Jameson said.

"I'm just glad he was finally ready to settle down," Gwendolyn said, ignoring him. "I can't tell you how happy Steven and I are to have you as part of our family."

Jameson pushed his chair back and stood. "I'll get us some more wine."

Jameson was coming up from the wine cellar when he saw Grandpa Charles coming in the opposite direction.

"What's bothering you?" he said with a serious blue gaze.

"Nothing," Jameson said, startled by the question. "I mean, I've been thinking about the Samara woman but—" He stopped when his grandfather shook his head.

"No, something besides that. Something besides Granger and the ranch. You left rather abruptly when your mother was teasing you and your new bride."

"I just thought we should get more wine."

"Really?"

Jameson sighed and leaned against the wall. "If I said yes, you still won't believe me, will you?"

"I just want you to tell me the truth."

"I'm fine."

Charles nodded. "You look happy."

"I am," Jameson said, a little amazed to realize that his words were true. He hadn't felt like this in years. He liked playing this role with Brooke. He liked being her husband. His good mood dipped because he knew it was just a role and that one day soon it would end.

"Afraid it's not going to last?" Charles said, seeing Jameson's expression change.

I know it won't. "Things change."

"You know that can be a good thing. We feel safe when things stay the same, but growth is essential for life to go on."

Jameson smiled. "I know you've found some new happiness of your own," he said, referring to Polly Ann Wier, the widow his grandfather had brought to his wedding.

Charles grinned. "I have, but we're not talking about me. Brooke is happy, too, so that means you're doing something right. Don't worry so much. Enjoy what you have and don't let it slip away."

Jameson was thinking about his grandfather's words an hour later as everyone enjoyed a light dessert and an expensive after-dinner wine in the main room.

Wes and Lydia went off to snuggle together on the porch, Grandpa Charles went home to rest and Gwendolyn spent time with Brooke looking over the wedding album. Jameson took the opportunity to steal some time to talk to his father.

"I couldn't get much out of the Baileys."

"I'm not surprised. Few people are talking. Have you been approached yet?"

"For what?"

"Brooke's land. I spoke to Mitch and I know before you two married there was interest from buyers. I thought they might have contacted you."

He knew he couldn't tell his father about the will. "Not yet."

"That's a surprise. Do you know if she wants to sell?"

"She doesn't."

"That's a relief. You probably already discussed it before you got married. This is a really good deal for us. Is that what you were thinking about when you proposed?"

"Are we back to that? I already said my piece, but you can believe what you want to."

"I'm sorry. That was out of line. I guess these land deals have gotten to me more than I want them to. You know I love Granger and, somehow, seeing it get sold off feels personal. It gets me right here." He pounded his chest.

Wes came into the room. "What's all the whispering about?"

"Nothing that would interest you."

"Still worried about the investor," he guessed.

"You obviously don't think we have a reason to," Jameson replied.

"No. And Samara isn't as bad as you think."

"That's you're unbiased opinion, of course."

"You don't have to believe me."

"We were just talking about the Palmer land," Steven said as the atmosphere tensed.

"It's not all Brooke's. There's Meredith's side," Jameson said.

"Shouldn't be too hard to convince her to sell to you," Steven said.

Jameson nodded, hating feeling like a fraud. The Palmer land wouldn't be his anyway, but his father didn't need to know that.

Jameson was so lost in his thoughts he nearly jumped when a light hand tapped him on the shoulder. He turned and saw his sister, Laney.

"Could I talk to you a minute?" she whispered.

He nodded and they went into another room. "What's up?" he asked once they were alone.

"I need the name of a private investigator."

"What do you need an investigator for? Have you spoken to Mom and Dad?"

Laney waved his questions away. "I can't tell them."

"Why not?"

"It's personal. Please don't ask any more questions."

His gaze sharpened. "Are you in some kind of trouble?"

"Don't worry about me."

"How can I not worry if you're in trouble?"

She hugged herself and forced a smile. "I've got everything under control. I'm an Olympiad, remember?"

"You're my little sister first."

"All I need is the name of a private investigator. All you have to do is just give me the name."

* * *

That night Steven looked out at the stars.

"Something's bothering you," Gwendolyn said, coming up behind him.

"I think Jameson is hiding something from me."

"Why do you think so?"

"I spoke to him about the Palmer land and he didn't have the answers I'd expected from him."

"Maybe that's a good thing."

"What do you mean?"

"Maybe for the first time in his life he's not just thinking about the ranch but something more. He's a newlywed, remember?"

"I remember."

"And they look happy."

"Yes."

"Are you going to fault him for that?"

"No. But at first I thought I had one son who didn't care enough and another who cared too much."

"And now?"

"And now I don't know. I'm glad Wes has found Lydia and I want to believe him about Samara, but I can't. And although I know Jameson is concerned, he's not taking the steps I thought he would. Why wait to contact Meredith? Why hasn't he spoken to any of the buyers to let them know the Palmer land isn't for sale? He's usually much sharper than that."

"It could be he's in love."

Steven didn't reply; he wanted his wife to be right, but something bothered him. Ranching was expensive and seasonal. If the investor didn't want the land for that, what did he or she want it for, and how would that change the town he loved?

"What's wrong?" Brooke asked when they returned home.

Jameson set his keys aside. "Why should anything be wrong?"

"You're quiet."

He shrugged and then sat in the living room. "I just don't have anything to say."

Brooke took a seat beside him then reached out to touch him but changed her mind. "You're more quiet than usual."

He sighed. "I just have a lot on my mind."

"Has your family been giving you a hard time about me?"

He turned to her, surprised. "No, you heard my mother. She's glad you're part of the family."

"Does it bother you?"

"It is what it is. We both know what had to be done."

"But you have regrets," Brooke said.

"Like I said, I have a lot on my mind, and it doesn't have to do with you."

Part of her felt relieved and another part felt hurt. What could be more important than the false marriage they shared? What made him withdraw from her? She knew that a lot weighed on his mind, and she wished he trusted her enough to share his worries with her, but she knew he didn't, at least not yet. She couldn't push him because that could draw him further away. She'd felt conflicted about the evening. The Broward clan had been so warm to her and she hated being part of a lie. "Would you like a drink?" she asked Jameson, desperate to fill the silence.

His face brightened. "That's a good idea." He stood and grabbed his keys. "I'll see you later," he said, opening the door.

Brooke looked at him in dismay. "Where are you going?"

"The Shank."

Brooke watched him leave. When she'd asked him if he'd wanted a drink, she'd hoped he'd want to stay and have it with her.

Chapter 11

Matthew Rainey hated small towns. What he hated more were small towns located in the middle of nowhere, and Granger, Montana, fit that description. The place likely had more cows than people. He'd seen herds of them on his drive through a countryside that seemed as big and wide as an ocean. He liked the fast-paced life of the city. He knew how to wheel and deal there. An unhurried pace made him nervous. But he was on a mission. He had to make sure he didn't lose his prize client—Brooke Palmer. He hadn't taken her for the typical artistic, temperamental type, but her latest behavior had been troubling.

She was a gold mine but didn't know it. He was already making more money off of her than he should have, and thankfully, she was blind to it. He loved clients like that: individuals who left everything up to him and didn't ask too many questions. He just needed to stroke her ego a little more and get her back in line. She was his way out, hoping to make enough money off Brooke to ensure he could retire by the time he was fifty.

He drove up the winding driveway in front of the Granger Inn.

"Sorry, we're full," the attendant said.

Matthew didn't find the woman pretty, but she had a big enough chest to make a man forget about her face. If he hadn't been in such a rush, he would have tried to get her name.

"Enough with the jokes, honey," he said, lifting his gaze from her most interesting asset. "What are your rates?"

"I said we're full."

"How can you be *full?*" Matthew Rainey said, truly bewildered.

"You must not be from around here."

The statement didn't deserve a response. If he looked like he belonged there he would go out and kill himself. "How much do you want?"

"You're not the first to offer me money and I would take it, if we had a room, but ever since Samara Lionne came to town, it's been crazy."

"Samara Lionne, the actress?"

"Yes."

"What's she doing here?"

"I think she's planning to shoot some kind of movie here."

Damn. "Hmm. So, is there anywhere else I can stay for just one night?"

"Unless you know somebody, you'll have to find lodging somewhere out of town."

"Thanks." Getting out of town was tops on his agenda. Hopefully he could find Brooke fast and then leave. It was late evening, and he hadn't planned on speaking to Brooke until tomorrow, but maybe he could gain Brooke's sympathy and spend one night at her place.

Before heading to the address he had for Brooke, Matthew stopped at the Shank of the Evening Saloon. He was hungry and never made key decisions on an empty stomach. He ordered his food then glanced around, wondering how he'd ended up there in the first place. Then he saw another man who looked as out of place as he did. He had a light complexion with dark eyes and was wearing a suit. He looked like an outsider, just like him. Not some ranch hand. He was probably a lawyer or financial advisor, a man of business. He had a dark, ruthless quality to him and Matthew immediately ascertained that he wasn't a man one wanted to cross.

Matthew thought fast. He could be an important ally and Matthew wanted to impress him. He could be involved with Samara Lionne. Matthew liked the thought of having as many important contacts as he could gather. Maybe he could even sell some of Brooke's pottery to Samara. That would be a great marketing opportunity.

The place was noisy, but he wanted to catch the man's attention and let him know what a savvy businessman he was. He pulled out his cell phone and called his receptionist. "Yes, I just got here. I'm here to speak to Brooke Palmer," he said, speaking loud enough for the other man to hear. He shook his head. "I mean Broward."

"I know that," she said, sounding irritated. "You told me why you were going there."

"I have a lot of plans for her. She's a great money-maker." He saw the man's interest increase. *Victory.*

"What is wrong with you?" his receptionist said.

Matthew continued hoping she'd soon catch on and just play along. "You'd be surprised. You know how the people out here deal in cattle? Well, she's my cash cow. She has no idea how much I'm making off of her. Of all my clients, she's my most prolific and most successful. Before I met Brooke, I had a collection of so-so artists and wannabes. But once I saw her work, I knew I had found a treasure."

"Who are you trying to swindle now?" she asked with a laugh.

She'd caught on. Matthew saw the other man stand. "Talk to you soon," he said, then hung up.

"I couldn't help overhearing your call," the man said. Something about his intense stare made a shiver of fear slide up Matthew's spine, but he knew if he wanted to deal with the sharks of business, he couldn't show fear. "A man like you doesn't usually end up in Granger."

"I go wherever my clients are."

The man held out his hand. "And you are?"

"I'm Matthew Rainey."

The man sat. "And you work for Brooke Broward?"

Matthew laughed. "I wouldn't say I work *for* her. I'm her broker, but I see it as a partnership."

"Things must not be very lucrative having to deal with an unknown artist."

Matthew grinned. "That's where you're wrong. For me, she's my big ticket."

The man leaned back and smiled. "How did you manage that?"

"She leaves everything to me. The best thing for me is that she is so focused on what she's making, as an artist, she doesn't want to be bothered with the business end. Which works for me. I mean, when she signed with me, she didn't question my rate, and over the years, I've increased my percentage and she hasn't a clue."

"How'd you manage that?" the man asked with an edge of doubt.

Matthew recognized a challenge and was ready to take it. "Because I'm good. I know how artists are, whether they are singers, painters or potters, like Brooke, they don't have a mind for business. Now, I'm not totally ruthless, mind you. She's earning a decent income, and I have played a role in getting her work seen. It's just that, if she knew how much I get up front from some of the galleries where her work is displayed, she'd probably have a fit."

"You can't keep it up."

"I can and I have. Because she makes a good living, she's put me in charge of everything else. She even gave me full responsibility for her banking account. I plan to get power of attorney when I see her. Her husband is probably as dense as she is when it comes to dealing with city people."

"Impressive. So why are you here if everything is working so well?"

"She got married to some cowboy."

"And he's a problem?"

"Not yet, but he could be. She canceled a major show because of him. I can't let that happen again. I didn't think I'd find a smart and savvy guy like you out here in the boondocks. Are you a lawyer or something?"

"Or something."

Matthew realized that the man was being cagey, which must mean he was probably connected to the actress or one of the town's wealthy residents. Matthew handed him a card. "In case you're interested in a new upcoming talent."

The man took the card then stood. It was only after he left that Matthew realized he'd never gotten his name.

Later that evening, he found a room in a neighboring town and prepared for his meeting with Brooke. Early the following morning, Matthew drove to the BWB Ranch and whistled at the sight. The grass was an extraordinary green, and he wouldn't be surprised if they were growing money on the side. The house was even more impressive. He'd been expecting some small homestead, but what he saw looked like a palace. But when he checked it wasn't the address he was looking for. He drove further and saw another home equally impressive but not as grand. He continued up the long driveway, stepped out of the car and walked to the front door. The housekeeper led him to the main living room.

Matthew sat with an anticipation he hadn't had in years. He knew the idea he had in mind would change his life.

"Matthew, what are you doing here?" Brooke asked, coming into the room and taking a seat.

"I came to talk some sense into you, but first I've got some news for you."

"What?"

"You know Samara Lionne is here, right?"

"Yes, of course I do."

"Well, that is the kind of thing you should have told me about. But that's fine. It's my job to think about the things you don't. I'm planning on getting her to buy your work."

"Please don't. I—"

"Why not? I heard she's buying up property in the area and may shoot a movie here so why shouldn't she buy some Western pottery, too? She shouldn't be too hard to persuade. This is a great opportunity. Think of the publicity. Better yet, don't think. Just like everything else, leave this to me."

Brooke looked at Matthew in shock. She'd never seen him act this way before. She heard the front door open and then Jameson entered the room. He had a sharklike grin she'd never seen before. He was wearing his regular cowboy boots, jeans and shirt, but for some reason she imagined him with a gun holster ready to shoot. She glanced at Matthew and saw his eyes widen. She didn't know what was going on but decided to make an introduction anyway.

"Jameson, this is—"

"We've met," Jameson said, sitting down beside her and resting his arm around her shoulders. It was a gesture of possession she hadn't expected from him and she found it both thrilling and unnerving. He felt tense, like a predator eyeing its prey.

She turned to Matthew, who looked furious.

"Have you talked to him already?" he asked her.

"What are you talking about?" Brooke asked, confused by the intensity of Matthew's words and Jameson's cold gaze.

"You think you can steal one of my clients?" Matthew asked Jameson.

Jameson brushed a strand of hair from Brooke's cheek. His fingers were hot against her skin, but his eyes remained glacial. "I wouldn't do that to a smart man like you," he said in a hard tone. He raised an eyebrow. "You still haven't figured out why I'm here?" He sighed as if bored. "I can understand your confusion. I didn't look like this at the Shank because I'd just spent dinner at my parents' house and they like their guests to dress up. I went there to think about a few family issues. But I couldn't help overhearing you on the phone, especially since you spoke loud enough for me to. See, you were right to mention Brooke's name because that certainly got my interest."

Color drained from Matthew's face as he finally came to the conclusion Jameson expected him to.

Jameson held out his hand with a smile. "Sorry I didn't introduce myself before. I'm that cowboy you're worried about. Jameson Broward, Brooke's husband."

Chapter 12

"I don't think I've ever seen a grown man cry like that before," Brooke said to Jameson once Matthew had gone.

"You're not working with him again."

"He was the first person to show true interest in my work."

"Good for him, but I'm the second person and I plan to get you better representation. I'll have my lawyers look over the contract you signed with him."

"I trusted him."

"You wouldn't have known."

"You did."

"Only because he made it so obvious. You should have seen him at the saloon puffing himself up like a horny cock."

"Were you afraid he was here to try to buy some property?"

Jameson paused. Strange, but he hadn't even thought of that. Only weeks ago that would have been his first assumption. But the sight of a flashy Mercedes-Benz with Colorado plates only made him think of Brooke. The fact shook him. He'd thought of her before thinking of his land or the ranch.

How could he have been so careless? He should guard his heart more. But she'd already slipped inside with her sweet smile, her independent ways and her passion for art. He knew he loved her and that gave her power over him. Power he was afraid to release. She didn't have to know, and he'd never tell her.

"Jameson? Is something wrong?"

"No, I…uh was just thinking about what I need to tell the lawyer."

Jameson could hardly sleep that night. He didn't want to be in a one-sided relationship again. Brooke was young and, as agreed to in their agreement, would be free in a year. Based on what he'd heard from her broker, Jameson knew Brooke would be able to manage her homestead from the proceeds of her work. There would be no reason for her to want to stay and continue to work in her studio while teaching their children how to make pottery. Damn, she even had him thinking about starting a family. She'd get bored just like Meredith. He was a rock and she was a cloud and, in time, he knew she'd pass out of his life.

* * *

Brooke couldn't sleep either. She'd seen Jameson rope a calf, but she'd never seen him rope in a man. She was still amazed by how Jameson had handled Matthew. She could understand why the BWB continued to be so prosperous. The men in charge were smart. But what she found most attractive was the fact that Jameson looked out for her. She liked how he introduced himself as her husband. For a sweet second, it had sounded real. As if he were laying claim. Instead of being offended or feeling sad, she'd felt glad. She only wished it was real.

Brooke and Jameson were finishing lunch together when they heard a loud squealing from outside. They both looked out the window and saw an old sedan coming up the drive with Cecelia in the driver's seat. They both went out to meet her.

"I hope you didn't pay more than a nickel for that thing," Jameson said as Cecelia locked her car.

"Don't make fun. I got it for a good price and the man said only a few adjustments need to be made. He's had this car in his family a long time. His mother used to only drive it to the grocery store and to church."

"Give me his name."

"Why?"

"So I can wring his neck."

Cecelia turned to Brooke. "What do you think?"

"I don't know much about cars," Brooke said, not wanting to hurt the older woman's feelings.

Jameson walked around the car, looking at it as if it were a dead carcass. "I'm surprised you made it up the drive. Why didn't you call me first before buying this thing?" He held out his hand for the car keys. "And if you say you didn't want to bother me, you'll make me angry."

Cecelia handed him the keys and watched him open the car and pop the lid. "I wanted to do it on my own. I felt so stupid after the Jeep fiasco. I've been using Brooke's car for errands, but I needed to replace my Jeep. I know it looks bad from the outside, but so did Royal Thunder when you first got him here, and through your tender care and attention, he's doing great now."

"What happened to the money you got from the car manufacturer?"

"My sister needed help with her mortgage and my brother needed a new transmission, plus I always like to have extra money put away in case of an emergency."

Jameson looked under the hood. "Cece, if this thing were a horse I'd have to take it out and shoot it." He slammed the hood shut. "And I'd shoot it twice. I don't want to see you in this again." He folded his arms. "How much did you pay for it?"

"I'm not going to tell you because you'll only make fun of me."

"I won't make fun of you."

Cecelia shook her head. "I'm still not telling you."

"At least give me a price range."

She shook her head again.

"Can you tell me?" Brooke said.

Cecelia thought for a moment then whispered something in Brooke's ear. Brooke looked surprised then chagrined. "Okay. Let me see what we can do."

"How can I do anything if I don't know what price range you're looking for?" Jameson said.

"I'll help you," Brooke said.

"I want something used and dependable," Cecelia said, looking hurt.

Jameson opened his mouth to respond, but Brooke shot him a glance that stopped him. "You can trust us."

"So how much did she spend?" Jameson asked as he and Brooke drove to a dealership outside of town.

"Promise you won't tease her if I tell you?"

"It's that bad?"

"What do you think?"

"I hope she spent less than a thousand."

Brooke sighed and stared out the window.

"Two thousand?"

Brooke rubbed her nose and still refused to look at him.

"Three?" Jameson said in a grave voice.

Brooke lightly tapped his leg as she would an agitated horse. "You don't want to know."

"Yes, I do," Jameson said, pounding the steering wheel. "I want to know how much she paid and the name of the bastard who sold her that piece of crap so that I can start making him walk a little funny."

"I do, too, but she feels bad enough, so don't make her feel worse. Let's just get her a new car and forget this ever happened. How long will it take before we reach the dealership?"

"We're not going to a dealership. The car's already

been bought. I had a friend take care of things. It will arrive tomorrow."

"I thought you didn't have any friends."

"I said I have *few* friends." He shook his head. "Sometimes I wonder if you ever listen to me."

Brooke looked around. "Then what are we doing out here?"

"Going for a drive. I thought it would be nice if Cecelia thought we really made an effort."

"Sometimes I forget you're a Broward and that your reputation and money make life easy."

"Sometimes."

"Most times."

"My money and reputation didn't make your sister stay," Jameson said in a low voice.

Brooke fell silent, not knowing what to say, bewildered that he would even bring up the subject.

"There are a lot of things I can buy and other things I can't. It's those intangible things that make everyone equal."

"You have the respect of your ranch hands, the loyalty of your house staff and the love of your family. Not many men could say the same."

"And what about you?"

Brooke's heart rate quickened. "What about me?"

She noticed his knuckles become white as he gripped the steering wheel. "Never mind," he said in a harsh voice. "I shouldn't put you on the spot like that. I don't even know why I brought it up. I could have proved my point another way. The last thing I want is for you to feel sorry for me."

"I don't," she said, feeling a little breathless. "Do you feel sorry for me?"

Jameson shot her a glance. "Why would I?"

"Because of the situation I put you in."

"Your father did that, not you." He released one grip on the steering wheel. "What we're doing makes sense, so don't feel guilty about it."

But she did feel guilty and saddened that he still saw her as an obligation. But she didn't want to talk about it anymore. "So where are we going again?"

"Nowhere in particular."

"Then can I drive?"

"Sure." Jameson pulled over to the side and they switched places. Brooke was surprised by how quickly he'd given over control. Most men hesitated in similar situations. They drove in silence for a few miles, and when Brooke glanced over at Jameson he was fast asleep. She smiled, pleased by his trust in her. She had once dated a guy who acted like a driving instructor every time she was behind the wheel. She liked Jameson's show of faith in her, or perhaps he was just too tired to complain.

"Are you going to keep staring at me or start looking at the road?" Jameson asked, his eyes still closed.

Brooke released a dramatic sigh. "And here I thought you weren't going to complain about my driving."

"I'm not complaining about your driving." He opened his eyes and looked at her. "I just want to know what you're thinking. Are you unhappy about something?"

"No. I didn't mean to stare, but I couldn't help it. I thought you were asleep. You looked so peaceful."

He laughed. "And I usually don't?"

"Not like that."

And she meant it. Away from the ranch he seemed more relaxed, more accessible, less preoccupied. She had a crazy desire to keep driving to another state. To show him that life was about so much more than the BWB. She wanted to kidnap him and tell him how much she loved him and that, if he gave himself the chance, he could learn to love her, too. But she knew that was only a young girl's fantasy and she was a woman now.

"You look more peaceful, too."

"I do?"

"Yes. I guess we both have a lot on our minds."

He was right and she knew that neither of them would tell the other what they were. She stared ahead and saw a large sign advertising free puppies.

"Did you ever get a new one?" Jameson asked.

"What?"

"When Radar died, did you get another working dog or pet?"

Brooke swallowed, touched. "I can't believe you remember his name."

"I also remember how sad you were."

"I never thought I'd get over him, but slowly I did."

"So did you?"

"No."

"Would you like one?"

Brooke bit her lip. "I don't think we should."

"Why not?"

Because she didn't want to buy something with him.

Something that would remind her of their time together. "We're both so busy."

"A good working dog always comes in handy."

"I don't want a puppy and I don't want to talk about it anymore." She turned the car around and headed back in the direction of home.

Jameson sent her an odd look, and nodded. "Fine."

Chapter 13

Cecelia squealed with the delight at the sight of her new car. Jameson had had the car dropped off in town, where he and Brooke could pick it up and drive it to the house.

"I still think you should tell her the truth," Brooke said, feeling uneasy with Jameson's plan of deception.

Jameson handed her the keys. "She won't accept it otherwise. She's a proud woman and she'll see it as charity."

"And it's not?"

"No, it's a gift. She deserves it. I don't ever want her worrying about her car again. I just need you to drive it to the house. If someone else does, she'll get suspicious."

"She has a right to be suspicious."

"She has the right to a car that will last. Trust me."

"I don't like being devious."

"Then let me be. You don't have to say anything."

And Brooke didn't utter a word when Jameson brought Cecelia out of the house to look at the car. The moment Brooke saw the awe on Cecelia's face she knew why Jameson had done it his way. Some of her uneasiness melted away.

"You two are the best," Cecelia said. "I'm the luckiest woman in the world." She ran her hand along the side of the car. "It's looks brand-new."

"It practically is," Brooke said.

Jameson nudged her.

Cecelia patted her chest. "How much did you pay for it?"

"Just an arm and a leg," Brooke said.

"What?"

Jameson stood in front of Brooke. "Don't worry about the price. We had to bargain with the dealership, that's all."

Cecelia hesitated. "You've both done so much for me already. I really shouldn't accept this."

"But you will." Jameson opened the car door. "Get in."

Cecelia needed no further persuasion. She got inside and lovingly ran her hand over the steering wheel and dashboard. "It even has that new-car smell. What used car lot did you go to?"

"Jameson Auto," Brooke said, darting from behind Jameson.

"What was that?" Cecelia asked. "Jameson what?"

Jameson covered Brooke's mouth. "Brooke's just toying with you. We went to some place out of town. I doubt you'd know it." He lowered his voice to a whisper that only Brooke could hear. "I thought I told you to be quiet."

She just blinked at him.

"Oh, it's… Wait." Cecelia squinted at the speedometer. "It's hardly been driven."

Jameson swore. "I knew I was forgetting something."

Cecelia jumped out of the car and pointed at him. "You got me a new car!"

Jameson sighed. "You make that sound like it's a bad thing."

"But this is too much." She slammed the car door shut. "I told you to get something used and dependable."

"I used it, and Brooke thinks it's dependable."

Cecelia turned to Brooke, stunned. "You were in on this, too?"

"He forced me."

"Yes, that sounds like him. I want a used car that I can afford. I already work for you I don't want to feel like I owe you extra."

"It's a gift."

"For what? Doing my job?"

"No, for being there for me when few people were. I know I don't say much and when I first hired you I thought it would just be employer and employee. But you're like family to me. While others kept trying to tell me how to run my life, you left me alone and didn't judge me and you still don't, and I appreciate that. I just want to thank you."

Cecelia's eyes filled with tears.

Jameson hung his head. "Don't embarrass me by crying."

"I can't help it. That's the sweetest thing I've ever heard you say."

Brooke gently shoved him forward.

He turned to her, surprised. "What?"

"Go and give her a hug," Brooke said under her breath.

"Really?"

"Yes," she hissed.

Jameson hugged Cecelia. "Now stop crying."

"I will, but next time don't spend so much money. Just tell me how you feel."

"You know I'm not good with words."

She playfully patted him on the cheek. "You do well enough." She held up her new car keys. "Now let's take this baby for a spin!"

"Why didn't you tell me?" Brooke asked Jameson that night after dinner as they sat in the family room watching TV.

"Tell you what?"

"Why you bought a new car for Cecelia."

Jameson shrugged, but she saw red stain his cheeks. "No reason."

A grin spread on Brooke's face. "You're blushing."

"No, I'm not," Jameson said, rubbing his chin and keeping his gaze on the screen. "I just don't like being fussed over."

"I know why."

He turned to her. "Why?"

"You're a softy and you're afraid that will ruin your reputation."

"I'm not a softy."

"Uh-huh. That's why you pay for malnourished horses so you can nurse them back to health and buy new cars for your staff when you don't have to."

"Do we really have to watch this?" Jameson said, frowning at the image of reporters and cameras on TV preparing for Samara Lionne's upcoming press conference.

"Yes. Aren't you curious what she has to say?"

"I hope she makes it brief."

Samara didn't, but what she had to say was riveting. She revealed that in addition to purchasing several parcels of land in the town, she had purchased Wes Broward's property and was in talks with Meredith Palmer to buy her half of the Palmer ranch. "I am fully committed to the town of Granger," she said. "I understand that some locals would prefer to keep Granger low profile, and I would like to ask you, the press, to respect their wishes. I plan to hold a big party next month where you can take all the photos you want. Until that time, I hope you will respect the privacy of my new neighbors. Thank you."

"I don't like her interest in the Palmer ranch," Jameson said.

"But she sounds sincere."

Jameson nodded. "She doesn't seem as bad as I thought."

"I wonder if we've misjudged her."

* * *

Brooke thought about Samara's press conference the next day as she walked around the ranch looking for some new inspiration. She stopped when she saw a brown dog sitting near the stables. Moments later she saw Jameson come out of the stables and shake hands with Frank. Both men looked up at her and started to wave, then they must have seen the look of thunder on her face. Frank made a quick exit as Brooke marched up to Jameson.

"What is that?" she demanded.

"Do you really need me to answer that?"

"Yes, I do."

"It's a dog."

"And what is it doing here?"

"It's ready to work. It's young and I'll train it for—"

Brooke shoved him back hard. "You arrogant bully!"

Jameson stumbled back a few feet, more out of shock than the force of her weight. "What's wrong?"

"I told you I didn't want a dog! Did you have cotton in your ears or something?"

He frowned. "I thought you didn't want the hassle of training a puppy."

"And you think you know what's best for me?"

"No, but I remember how much you cared about Radar and—"

"Thought you could replace him?"

"Stop putting words in my mouth. If you'd stop shouting and allow me to finish a sentence for once, maybe we can start communicating."

"I don't want to talk to you." She turned.

Jameson grabbed her wrist and spun her around. "Well, that's too bad."

"I don't want you buying me things. Flowers are fine, but nothing more. Forcing you to marry me was enough. I don't want to feel beholden for anything else."

"You didn't force me to do anything, and I thought you said we were friends. Hell, we're lovers and lovers can do things for each other."

Brooke shook her head, frustrated. "You don't understand. I don't want anything that will remind me of—" She stopped before she said too much.

"Of what?" Jameson pressed her.

Of you! The thought of leaving him already pained her. She couldn't bear having a dog that would remind her every day of what she'd lost. It would be like experiencing the death of Radar all over again. "Either send him back or keep him for yourself. I don't want him."

"Fine, I'll keep him, but if you change your mind…"

"I won't."

Jameson gently jabbed her in the shoulder. "Stop interrupting me."

She jabbed him back. "Then stop saying things that annoy me."

"How can I know what annoys you," he said, jabbing her again.

Brooke jabbed him harder. "If you'd listen, you'd find out."

"I do listen. You just don't make any sense."

"I always make sense."

"Are you still mad at me?"

"Yes."

"Then I'm going to really make you angry."

"Why?"

Jameson started to back away from her with a grin on his face. "Because I got two."

"What?"

Jameson began to laugh then saw the look on Brooke's face and turned and ran so fast that his hat blew off.

She chased after him. Jameson was faster, but Brooke had more endurance. Soon the ranch hands began cheering them on. Those for Jameson shouted, "Keep going, man. Don't let her catch you!" Those rooting for Brooke shouted, "You're gaining on him. Don't give up."

Steven, drawn by the noise, joined the group. "What's going on? Who's that running from Brooke?" he asked Frank. "A new ranch hand that got on her bad side?"

Frank laughed. "No, that's your son."

Steven frowned. "That doesn't look like Wes."

"That's because it's Jameson."

"Jameson?"

Frank laughed even harder at the shocked expression on Steven's face. "Yes, your eldest. The one we all thought had forgotten how to smile."

Steven stared at Jameson again, barely recognizing him. Even though he was a few yards away, Steven could see his profile and it didn't have the hard edge that he'd grown used to. His son looked so young and carefree again, reminding him of when he was five and could hardly be kept in the house. He was always rushing through his breakfast and then racing outside to play with the farm animals. Gwendolyn always despaired of keeping him clean. She once joked that she should just let him run around naked like a wild animal. He dashed from one part of the ranch to the other without losing enthusiasm. And he was always full of questions. "And what's this, Dad?" Or performing some feat and demanding attention. "Watch me, Dad." And then he'd do something that would make Gwendolyn want to scream and Steven laugh. Finally, he saw the man that young boy had grown into before heartbreak had shut him down. "I don't believe it," he said in a choked voice, blinking back tears.

"Me neither," Frank said, sobering, sensing the other man's amazement. "But it's real. Brooke has really brought out a good side to him."

Steven didn't feel anything but pride as he watched his son, the tightening in his chest easing a bit. He'd come over to Jameson's house to discuss more rumors about the private investor, but that didn't matter now. In the past he'd wanted his son to focus on the ranch and nothing else. He'd encouraged it, despite his wife's protests saying that work always helped a man get his life in order. But he'd helped his son make the ranch his life and now he'd help him separate the two. He wouldn't have Jameson worry as he did.

If Jameson had known his father was watching, he would have stopped running instantly. But because he didn't he ran nearly five more minutes until the crowd was in a frenzy. Jameson eventually stopped and turned around with his hands in the air in surrender. "I'm sorry."

Brooke didn't stop. She ran up to him and tackled him to the ground before she tried to saddle him. He rolled away, out of her grasp.

"I said I was sorry," he said, but his eyes danced with humor.

"But you don't mean it?"

"I do."

"That's not good enough."

Jameson's lip twitched.

Brooke narrowed her eyes. "You really think this is funny?"

He bit his lip. "You should have seen the look on your face." He burst into laughter.

Brooke watched him amazed. She'd never seen him laugh before. His laughter made him look years younger and more carefree and she liked the sound of it. It was free, fun, sexy and contagious. Before she knew it, Brooke was laughing, too.

"I'm going to get you," Brooke said, wiping tears from her eyes.

Jameson stumbled to his feet, sobering, then held his hand out to her. "I'll watch myself," he said as he effortlessly lifted her up. "Do you forgive me?"

She playfully punched him in the chest. "Only if you'll send them back."

"Are you sure? Can I keep just one?"

"No."

"Please?"

She folded her arms. "It's your house, so you can do whatever you want."

"True, but I don't want you to be unhappy."

Brooke let her hands fall. "Fine, keep one. Keep them both if you want to."

Jameson drew her into his arms and kissed her.

Brooke tried to shove him away before he completely made her forget how angry she'd been with him. "What are you doing?"

He locked his arms around her waist and flashed a lazy smile. "You know what I'm doing." He placed a kiss on her neck.

"Stop it."

"What? Kissing you or holding you?"

"Both."

Jameson released her, his dark gaze searching her face. "You're really that angry?"

Not anymore. "Yes."

"How can I make it up to you?" he asked. And at that moment, to Brooke, Jameson looked young and vulnerable and wonderful. Like a man who cared about pleasing his wife.

Brooke had to bite the inside of her mouth to keep from smiling. "I'll think of something."

Later that night Steven told his wife what he'd seen and she couldn't believe it either. Three times she asked, "Are you sure it was Jameson?" And she'd shake her head in disbelief, until tears of joy streamed down her cheeks when he confirmed it. And he'd held her and they'd both cried with joy that their son was back. They were both happy that the wedding had been real and that Brooke was the perfect woman for him.

Steven also thought of his father, Charles, and silently thanked him for stopping him from saying anything to Jameson at the wedding. He was glad he'd kept his suspicions about Jameson's true motivation to himself. He felt ashamed that he'd judged him so harshly.

Jameson named the dogs Ben and Trevor. Ben eagerly accepted any new job he was given, whereas Trevor gravitated to Royal Thunder, and the horse appeared to feel the same. Trevor would sit in front of the horse, and Royal Thunder would nibble on its fur, as if grooming it. Jameson didn't want to give him back. The dog reminded him a little of Brooke. It was smart and caring. He'd really thought she'd be happy about the dog. A good cow dog was always helpful on a ranch. But maybe she had different plans for her ranch that she hadn't told him about. No, he didn't think she'd be that devious. As she said, she didn't want anything more from him. Just his last name for a while and a roll in the sack when the mood was right. He'd have to be satisfied with that.

Two days later Brooke had the perfect idea of how she could get back at Jameson for getting the two dogs. She walked into Jameson's study carrying a small clay bowl. "Here."

Jameson frowned at it. "What is this?"

"Your bowl. You made it, remember? I thought you should paint it, too." She folded her arms. "I couldn't think of another way to get back at you for the dog incident, but I'm trying to be nice."

Jameson shook his head. "No, I'll stick to what I do well. Besides, I don't want to bother you. Come up with something else. I'm willing to wash your car."

"No, I want you to do this. Besides, you don't bother me. I like having you around. I know you enjoyed making this."

Jameson stared at the bowl for a long moment then shook his head again. "Please, do whatever you want with it. You can throw it away if you want to."

Brooke couldn't do that. It would be like throwing away a wonderful memory. His dismissive words hurt. Would he be able to "throw away" what they had together so easily?

"I've been talking to another broker about your work," he continued. "And the lawyers have looked over the contract. You'll be set up well when our year is up."

Does our year have to end? "Thanks."

"Don't thank me. You're the one with the talent. You don't need me."

"Yes, I do."

Jameson turned to her with a look of surprise. "What?"

"A person always needs a good friend." She held up the bowl. "Come on, it'll be fun."

"I told you, I'm not very creative."

Brooke rested a hand on her hip. "Over the past several weeks you've been very creative." Jameson knew what she was referring to, and it wasn't about working with clay.

"I mean I'm not artistic."

She grinned. "That, too." She looked around the study. "Of course, if you want to move back in here that's fine."

Jameson stiffened, quickly understanding her threat. "That's blackmail."

Brooke rested the bowl on the desk and lowered her voice. "It's revenge."

"You've got a nasty streak."

"I can be just as surly as you if I want to."

Jameson believed her, but he also remembered the wayward thoughts he'd had when he'd made the bowl. He was already more attracted to her than he wanted to be. He didn't want to spend more time with her than he had to. He didn't want to make a fool of himself. He held out his hand. "I can wax your car, too."

"You'll probably just hire someone to do it for you."

"No, I'll do it myself."

"With your shirt off?"

"If you want," he said, eager to get her to agree.

Brooke shook her head then pointed to the bowl. "Sorry, but I'd prefer to see you finish this."

Jameson sighed then stood. Together they drove over to the studio.

While Jameson painted, Brooke tried to focus on her own work, but she couldn't help stealing glances at him.

Jameson gave a low growl. "You're doing it again."

"What?"

"Staring at me."

"I can't help it. I like what I see."

"Hmm…me completely out of my element. You want to start laughing now?"

"You're doing fine."

Jameson set his brush down. "I'm done."

Brooke looked at the bowl, which he had painted brown, green and blue. She smiled. "A Montana horizon?"

He returned her expression. "Yes."

Brooke lifted her gaze to his face. "Your only true love, right?"

His eyes met hers, and he stared at her with an intensity she'd never seen before. It made her breath catch and her heart beat faster.

"Listen, Brooke, I can't—" His cell phone rang. He glanced down. "Sorry, I have to take this." He answered then listened and swore. "I'll be right there." He disconnected.

"What's wrong?"

"Some cows got loose through a broken fence in the eastern quarter. And two hands are out with the flu so we're shorthanded." He rushed out the door of the studio.

Brooke gripped her hands into fists. *Damn cows have ruined a perfect moment.* What was Jameson about to say? He couldn't what? Love her? Feel anything more for her than lust? Brooke glanced down at the bowl, saw the colors of the Montana horizon and knew she could never compete with such a mistress.

He was getting too attached to her, Jameson thought as he worked on repairing the fencing. They'd managed to get the cattle back and the crisis was over, but he still felt on edge. He was exhausted, but he didn't want to go home yet. He already knew he'd miss her when she left. He needed to prepare himself for it. He'd stay out of her studio. Maybe spend more time in the study than in the master suite. They were starting to feel more and more like a real married couple and he didn't like that. That wasn't how it was supposed to turn out. It was dangerous and foolish to believe his own lie. He wiped sweat from his brow then glanced up and saw a slender figure a few yards away working on another part of the fence. Brooke.

Jameson finished what he was doing then walked over to her.

"What are you doing?"

"Helping. You said you were shorthanded. I know what needs to be done." She pressed a finger against his lip. "Don't argue. Let's just finish this."

Jameson started to smile but frowned instead. Damn, he was really going to miss her when she left, but he'd never ask her to stay.

Chapter 14

Brooke would never have described herself as a jealous woman until she saw the dark-haired, Native American beauty flirting with Jameson that afternoon. The two stood in the driveway, and Brooke watched through the living room window as the woman playfully slapped Jameson on the arm, making him smile. Brooke flexed her fingers. She wanted to be the only woman who could make him smile. Who could make him relax, to make him want more. Who was that woman? And why was she so comfortable with him when everyone knew that Jameson hardly looked at women? She would find out, but she didn't know how. She didn't want to just walk up to them and come up with a phony reason to join the conversation or give Jameson a chore he'd either already completed or would hold off for later. Maybe she was making too much of it.

"She is a looker, isn't she?" Cecelia said behind her.

"Yes," Brooke reluctantly admitted. But it wasn't just her looks that struck her; it was the way the woman carried herself. She appeared to be a confident woman, around Jameson's age, with an affinity to Jameson that made Brooke wonder about her more. Did they have a past together?

"At one point I thought that something would happen between them," Cecelia said. "They have so much in common. But I didn't know about you, of course," she quickly added. "I'm sure you two will get on well."

"Who is she?"

Cecelia looked at her in surprise. "You mean he hasn't told you? She's the owner of the horse rescue organization."

"Oh," Brooke said, remembering Jameson talk about the rescue service he'd first approached with Royal Thunder. "How long have they worked together?"

"Years, but you have nothing to worry about. Jameson is a trustworthy man."

Brooke plastered on a smile, ashamed that Cecelia could sense her unease. "I'm not worried about that. I was just curious."

Cecelia sent her a long look. "It's none of my business, but I know when there's tension."

Brooke's smile fell as heat burned her cheeks. She'd sensed a shift in her relationship with Jameson but hadn't thought anyone else would notice it. After their time in the studio, their interaction had been cordial but stilted. She'd tried to guard her heart as she watched Jameson with the dogs and he'd kept them far from her as he'd promised, but the companionable relationship she'd hoped to have with him had become strained. She had many more months to go, though, so she had to keep up appearances. "No, we're fine now."

"The first married fight is always the hardest, but it gets better from there. He shouldn't have gotten those dogs without telling you, but I'm sure it won't happen again."

"I'm past that."

"Good, grudges are like weeds. They can strangle a garden. So can feelings of jealousy."

"But I'm not…" She stopped when Cecelia sent her a knowing look. "Okay, maybe a little. I mean, look at her."

"I have, but remember that he married *you*."

Only because I forced him to. "I know."

"Instead of standing there burning with curiosity, why don't you go over and introduce yourself?"

"I would feel like I'm intruding."

"That doesn't sound like the woman who helped me douse a car fire or care for a sick horse." Cecelia went to the door and opened it. "Go and say hello. I'll make sure refreshments are ready."

Brooke sighed, knowing that Cecelia was determined and wouldn't buy any excuse Brooke tried to come up with.

She walked outside and half hoped that the woman would be getting into her car by the time she reached them, but neither Jameson nor the woman seemed ready to part company. Brooke took a deep breath then approached them. "Hello, I'm Brooke. I couldn't help seeing you out here. Would you like to come in for some refreshments?"

With hazel eyes and flawless skin, the woman was even more stunning up close. Brooke half expected her to flatly refuse when she sent a look to Jameson. "I wouldn't want to take up too much of your time," she said.

Jameson shrugged. "Come on. You know you're always welcome."

Minutes later the three of them were sitting in the living room eating crackers and cheese.

"I still don't know your name," Brooke said.

"Linda Bearclaw," she said with no elaboration.

The silence stretched, but Jameson seemed in no hurry to fill it. Brooke saw the uncertain look Linda again sent to Jameson. Something was going on between them. She wasn't sure she wanted to know what, but she would face the truth.

"Okay, why are you here?" Brooke asked. She regretted how tactless her question sounded, but she had to know

"You tell her," Jameson said.

Linda shook her head. "I told you that it's not my place. Besides, it's your idea."

"It will sound better coming from you. Brooke doesn't always like my surprises," Jameson said with a sheepish grin.

Brooke was confused. "What's going on?"

"Jameson has a great idea that I think will really help us—" Linda started.

"But I said it was just an idea and I haven't convinced her yet," Jameson interrupted.

"So convince her now."

"Convince me of what?" Brooke demanded, tired of their secrecy.

When Jameson didn't respond, Linda leaned forward and said in an eager voice, "To help the horse rescue."

Brooke blinked. She'd imagined a number of things that Linda could say, but that wasn't one of them. "Me help the rescue agency? How?"

"We're holding a fund-raiser for the rescue and we need items to auction. Jameson thought you could donate maybe two of your pottery pieces so that people could bid on them, and whatever they agree to pay, he'd match it. Jameson figured that way you could get exposure for your work and help raise money plus add a level of class to the auction. Everyone knows that pottery is big in this state, and to get your name attached to a worthy cause would add sophistication to the event."

"Oh, you mean using the Broward name?"

Linda frowned. "No, not just that. Of course having a Broward involved would be helpful, but Jameson has told me that your work is known throughout the state and that you'll soon have a gallery online for buyers."

Brooke sent Jameson a look, but he was staring out the window. "He said that?"

"Yes, he said you're one of the best potters he's ever met. So would you be willing?"

"Of course," Brooke said, amazed by the praise of

her work. She'd known Jameson had respected her as an artist but not to this level.

Linda smiled. "Thank you. This will mean so much to us. I'll send you the logistics later today."

They chatted some more about the fund-raiser then Brooke stood. "I'm going to see what I have in my studio. This discussion has gotten me so inspired, I may create something special especially for the event."

"That would be great!" Linda replied.

Linda watched Brooke leave then looked at Jameson. She remembered the first time she'd set eyes on him, when he'd come to the organization to ask what help they needed. The Browards were known for their interest in horses, and she hadn't been surprised by his offer of help. What had surprised her was his intelligence and his "don't mess with me" attitude. She would have slept with him if he had ever given her the chance. But he hadn't, and now he was married so she knew that opportunity was gone. "See, was that so hard?" she said. "I don't know why you didn't think that she would go for it."

"You don't understand her the way that I do."

"You think too hard sometimes."

"Maybe, but not this time. She said yes to you, not to me."

"I doubt you ever have a problem getting a woman to say 'yes' to you. But I never thought I'd see you married. Funny how you never mentioned anything about her. But you are a man of secrets."

Jameson rubbed his chin and didn't reply.

"She's a little young, isn't she?" Linda said, determined to get him to say something.

"She's not that young."

"True. I guess I'd always hoped you'd like your women a little more seasoned. But I guess once a woman hits thirty the men stop looking."

"Men never stop looking. You'll find the right man one day."

She made a face. "I knew you'd say that."

"You know I'm right."

"So, how did you meet?"

"I wonder why everyone keeps asking us that question? Does it matter?"

"People always enjoy a good love story. You're avoiding the question."

"Yes. I'm not very interesting. I get married and then all of a sudden my personal life becomes the topic of conversation."

"You can't blame people. Nobody expected you to have a personal life. I thought I knew all I could about you. I thought I knew things even your family didn't know, like you helped us rescue horses and helped our mission. But I didn't know about her. *Nobody* knew about her. Why was she such a big secret?"

"Because of this. Because of your speculation about her age and even who her family is."

"Yes, I'd heard about her sister and how things had ended between you two."

Jameson frowned. "I like you better when you talk about horses."

Linda laughed. She couldn't share that it had felt like

a betrayal when he'd gotten married without telling her. Not that they were close, but she'd felt that she'd known him like no one else. She'd flirted with him and he'd let her, and it had been a fun relationship she'd hoped could have developed into something else. He was a sexy man, but she knew that she could never get past the wall he'd put between him and everyone else. It seemed that Brooke had managed to get past that wall and she had to applaud her for that. She wondered what the secret had been. What his weakness was. "I really like her," she said. "Even though I know my opinion doesn't matter."

"Hmm."

"I'm happy for you. You two should become part of the horse rescue's board of directors. I think your idea will really make a difference for us. It's going to be the best fund-raiser we've had in years."

Jameson certainly hoped so. He sat in the family room after Linda had gone and wondered if using Brooke's work would be a good idea. If the auction didn't go as either woman planned, they'd both blame him. But he wasn't a defeatist. It would work, and this way he could make up for Brooke missing the Sugarloaf Craft Festival.

"Oh, is she gone?" Brooke asked, returning to the room with a bunch of papers under her arm.

Jameson glanced at his watch. "Yes, about twenty minutes ago."

Brooke sat down beside him. "Sorry I took so long.

I was just thinking of some ideas and started sketching—"

He took the papers from her. "These look good. Choose whatever one you want to work on."

"What was that about an online gallery?" Brooke said.

"What?" Jameson asked in an absent way as he stared at another sketch.

"Why did you mention me having an online gallery?"

Jameson shrugged. "I'm surprised that Rainey hadn't thought of that before. It seems like a good idea and another way artists can get their work seen."

"And I'm the best you've ever met?"

"You are."

Brooke sniffed. "Probably because you've never met a potter before."

He raised his brow. "Are you questioning my taste?" He pressed a finger against her lips before she could speak. "You're supposed to be flattered because I have excellent taste."

Brooke pushed his hand away. "What if no one places a bid on my work?"

He shook his head. "An artist never doubts her work. She can doubt the intelligence of her audience but never her work."

"And how do you know so much about artists?"

"It's not so different from what I do. I buy and sell to my customer. I know I'm good at what I do and you are, too."

"How did you meet her?"

He frowned. "Meet who?"

"Linda."

He started to smile. "Funny, she asked the same question about you."

"And what did you say?"

"Nothing. If you're curious about each other, you two should get together."

Brooke glanced down at her sketches. "She's a very beautiful woman."

"She's not my type."

Brooke lifted her head. "I didn't know you had a type."

I thought I'd made my type pretty obvious, Jameson thought but realized that maybe Brooke didn't want to see how he really felt.

Chapter 15

Brooke looked around her studio, not sure which pottery pieces would be the best for the auction. She'd only pretended to look earlier. When she'd left Jameson and Linda alone, she hadn't gone to her studio. She just walked around trying to figure out how she felt. How could Jameson have said all those things about her? And Linda seemed so impressed; she didn't want to disappoint them. She still had that fear as she looked at her artwork, although she was certain she'd just use one of her sketches to come up with something new. She really didn't want to let anyone down. She wanted to impress Jameson. She wanted to impress the Browards. She wanted the town of Granger to know how much she could contribute to this worthy cause. That she wasn't just Roy Palmer's daughter or Jameson's wife but a talented person in her own right. A person who commanded respect the way Gwendolyn and Laney did.

She turned when there was a light knock on the door, then Cecelia came into the room.

"Well?" she said.

"Well what?"

"Did you like her?"

Brooke smiled. "Don't pretend you weren't listening by the door."

"I don't eavesdrop," Cecelia said, looking offended.

"Not even a little?"

"Okay, maybe just a little, but I couldn't stay because I had to talk to the housekeeper. So what did you think?"

"I liked her."

"I knew you would."

"But she still makes me nervous."

"Why?"

"Because of what Jameson told her about my work. And now I have to find or create the right pottery pieces for the auction."

"Oh, yes, Jameson told me about that. It sounds wonderful. I think it's a great idea to donate some of your work to help raise funds for the rescue."

"Yes, it sounds like a great idea, but I want to make sure I can pull it off."

"Of course you can pull it off. You worked hard to get those items ready for that craft festival you had to miss. This would be close to that and also will help with promotion. I know you won't get paid for your pieces but—"

"I don't care about being paid. I care about representing myself in the right way. It was different when it was only my ego on the line, but now Linda, Jameson and all the horses depend on me bringing in enough money. What if it doesn't work? What if I don't raise enough money? What if no one bids at all?"

"Of course someone will bid. Your work is fabulous. I'll be there and so will all the people who care about you." She looked around the studio. "And I can tell from what I've seen that Jameson isn't just flattering you. I was married to a potter who worked with the indigenous clay found in this area of Montana."

"I didn't know that. Why didn't you tell me earlier?"

"It slipped my mind. Besides, I first thought that the private investor buying up land in this town was interested in the secrets this land holds."

"What secrets?"

"Well, on the far side of the property is where you can find the special clay, Precambrian Grecian shale. This shale, with three colors found together, cannot be found anywhere else in the whole state of Montana."

Brooke gasped in awe. She knew that Cecelia was talking about the shale she had heard about that was used to make calico clay. She'd learned about the shale while taking a course at Montana State University. A special process had to be used to keep the dark red, rich brown and creamy ivory separated. Then the clay was poured into molds, giving each sculptured piece a unique marbled or calico look. No two items looked alike. She hadn't been able to find that kind of shale after she had finished the university course.

"Are you sure some of that shale is here on the Broward property?"

"I'm pretty sure. There's an old map that we can look at." Cecelia disappeared into the family room and pulled out a rolled-up piece of paper.

They looked at the map. "Yes, there it is," Cecelia said excitedly.

"Let's go find it," Brooke said. It would be just the material she needed to make a magnificent piece in time for the auction. It was worth the adventure. They left early the next day and in their excitement forgot to leave a note for Jameson. They also did not see the ominous dark clouds off in the distance. They drove for several miles. Brooke had never seen this part of the Broward property. The Palmer property was much smaller. Although profitable, it did not have the extensive mountainous areas as the ones found on the Broward property. As Brooke drove, Cecelia was in charge of reading the map, which they followed closely. They soon found themselves driving on a long winding dirt road that ended in the front of a cave.

"This is it," Cecelia said. They parked the car and went inside the cave, carrying several bright flashlights. After walking for a few feet, they saw a wondrous sight. Right in front of her was the most incredible assortment of shale she had ever seen.

"I don't believe this," Brooke said. "It's amazing." She moved closer and ran her hand over the shale, fascinated and excited about their find. "It's like an artist's treasure trove."

"I know. If those investors found out about this—"

"I'm not telling anyone. Do the Browards know about the shale?"

"I don't know. I never heard anyone except my husband mention it. I didn't say anything because no one ever asked."

"I'll just take enough shale for the items I would like to make for the fund-raiser, that's all."

Brooke retrieved the items she had packed in the trunk of her car, then carefully collected the shale and put them in several waterproof containers she had packed for the trip. As she finished putting her equipment away it started to rain. She and Cecelia were packed and ready to go just as the downpour hit. They were in the car and driving back home when, within minutes, the dirty road was turned into a muddy river, dragging the car along with it.

"I'm so sorry about this," Cecelia said in a tense voice.

"What?" Brooke said, trying to sound calm, although she was worried about keeping a grip on the wheel and maintaining control of the car. It felt like it was gliding. "The rain? It's not your fault. I wanted to come, too."

"But I don't want there to be any more tension between you two. Jameson is going to be mad when he finds out I took you out here in this kind of weather."

"I'm not a child. I can take care of myself, and I don't know what you're talking about. What tension?"

Cecelia shot her a glance and frowned. "Don't play dumb with me. Ever since he got those two dogs I've noticed the distance between you two. But it doesn't matter now."

"Why?"

"Because we're going to die." Cecelia let out a stifled scream as the car began to swerve.

"No, we're not going to die." Brooke tightened her grip on the steering wheel as she felt the car begin to pull out from under them.

"Nobody knows we're out here."

Brooke couldn't maneuver the car well and they soon realized she was losing control and the water was pushing them forward. That's when she saw where the road fell away.

It had been a hard day. Jameson returned home that evening, hungry and tired. The house was oddly dark and quiet, and there was no note and no food on the warmer. He wasn't too surprised; he figured Brooke must be still in her studio preparing for the fund-raiser. He called Cecelia's number, but it went directly to voice mail. He called Brooke's cell phone and got her voice mail, too. That was strange. He couldn't reach either of them, so he called Frank.

"Have you seen Cecelia or Brooke?" he asked once Frank picked up.

"Yes. I saw them driving off early in the morning in the direction of the red cliffs."

"Thanks." Jameson put the phone receiver down. That was odd. With the kind of weather they were experiencing, he found their actions to be reckless. Especially for Cecelia. She knew that that part of the property was where slow-moving streams became raging rivers, especially during and following major rainstorms. Because of how rugged the area was, none of the cattle were ever taken through there. It was mountainous and dangerous and an easy place for someone who didn't know what they were doing to get lost. Jameson felt himself growing angry. Why did Brooke decide to go there without telling him what she was doing? And Cecelia should've known better. She should have left a note.

Maybe he was overreacting. Maybe Frank got it wrong and they just went shopping and he didn't need to worry.

But after another hour passed and the rain increased, Jameson's dark thoughts began to gather.

The rain had lightened but their troubles hadn't ended. Brooke swallowed, trying to keep her panic in check. The car sat in a precarious position: hanging off a semi-cliff, where the earth had just fallen away. Brooke knew she had to find a way to get out, but she was aware that any movement could make the car become dislodged and plunge them into the ravine below.

When the rain let up, Brooke had parked the car so that they could wait out the weather. Cecelia then stepped out to get something from the trunk, and the moment she did some of the soil gave way, taking the car partly over the edge, where it was now lodged, with only a large tree branch keeping it from toppling further.

Cecelia pulled out her cell phone and called Jameson while Brooke tried to think of an exit plan. "Where the hell are you?" Jameson demanded before Cecelia could speak.

In a trembling voice she told him the location. "We need to get help now. The car is hanging over a cliff, and Brooke's inside."

Cecelia half expected him to shout at her or swear. Instead his voice became ominously calm and he said, "We'll be there" before he disconnected.

Jameson knew he needed to get out there as fast as he could. He didn't have time to wait for the wilderness rescue team. He would have to see what he could do himself. He phoned Frank and told him what happened and that he needed to get as many of the available ranch hands as he could to come help. Then Jameson, Frank and a few helpers threw items they thought they would need in the back of two all-terrain vehicles and drove through the rain. By the time they reached Cecelia, she was frantically jumping up and down and pointing off in the distance.

"Oh, Jameson. I'm so sorry, I'm so sorry," she said, tears streaming from her eyes.

"Are you okay?" Jameson asked, in no mood to hear her apologies. He knew they didn't have any time to spare.

"I'm fine. But—"

"Where's the car?"

She pointed off to the side, where they could see Brooke's car hovering in a precarious position. Below the car, what once was a small stream was now a raging river, threatening to destroy everything in its way.

He could see Brooke inside the car, her face mirroring the horror she was feeling. She was still holding on to the steering wheel. Her eyes wide and fixed.

Frank swore. Jameson felt like swearing, too, but he had to stay focused. He couldn't let emotions rule him. He turned to his team, gave them instructions, then said, "Let's go."

The men immediately went into action. They were accustomed to these kinds of rescues, but they were usually rescuing a calf or cow, not a human being. Not Jameson's wife. They quickly found several large branches nearby and carefully pushed them under the car to create a canopy. Then they used heavy-duty rope to tie to the car to prevent it from falling any farther. Once they felt they had it secured, Jameson lay on his belly and inched his way slowly over the branches until he reached the driver's-side door.

"Now, Brooke, I need you to slowly, very slowly slide down to me."

"I can't," Brooke said, frozen in terror. She couldn't think straight. Fear prevented her from moving.

"Brooke, I need you to trust me."

Brooke watched as Jameson carefully opened the door, extending his hand up to her. "Just look at me. I'm here. It'll be all right." Brooke looked down at him, her heart pounding, and slowly slid out of the car seat and onto the branches below.

"Stay close to me. Don't make any sudden moves." Jameson helped Brooke inch by inch move closer and closer toward safety. Suddenly Frank reached out, grabbed her and pulled her to solid ground. Jameson came up close behind her.

Jameson reached out and held her close for a long time, but neither of them said a word, although they both had so much they wanted to say. The thought of losing her had scared him.

They could not do anything about retrieving her car. Five minutes after they reached safety, it broke loose and tumbled down into the ravine. Everyone stood still as the full realization that both Brooke and Cecelia could have still been in the car became crystal clear, and the two women realized how close they had come to death.

"If you'd wanted a new car, you could have just told me," Jameson said.

"I'm so sorry."

"I know." He lightly kissed her on the forehead, although he wanted to shake her for scaring him. "Let's go home."

Things changed between them after that day. They didn't talk about the incident, but it created a fissure between them like the sting of a paper cut. Neither could confess how shaken they'd been. Jameson couldn't admit how the stark fear of losing her haunted him. Brooke couldn't admit that she felt like a coward. She'd stared death in the face but still couldn't tell Jameson how she really felt about him. She couldn't let him know how much she wanted to repay him for all that he'd given her. Instead, the fear of disappointing him, of feeling like an obligation, weighed heavy on her and held her words back.

They made love that night, but for both it felt hollow, and neither would tell the other. So they let the lie they'd told the community—that they'd married for love—separate them, while they both tucked away their true feelings, never realizing how much damage their silence would cause.

Chapter 16

Two days later, as Brooke walked to her studio she saw Ben. He was tied to a post and stood still like a statue as his soulful brown gaze followed her. He wasn't usually tied so she guessed he'd done something wrong.

"You can look at me all you want, I'm not going to pet you," Brooke said. He was a handsome dog, and she was tempted to run her hand through his silky brown fur. She'd seen Cecelia take him on his daily walks and Jameson had used him with the cattle, so he'd gotten plenty of attention. He didn't need more. But for some odd reason, he called to her. "Okay, I'll give you a quick pat," she said, walking over to him. Ben's tail started to wag as if he understood her. She knelt down and stroked him and he licked her face. He had the exuberant energy of a young dog and reminded her of when her mother had bought Radar home. He'd licked her face exactly the same on the first day. Suddenly she remembered the scent of her mother's hair and the sound of her father's heavy boots in the mudroom as he took them off after a long day working on the ranch. Now they were both gone—the two people who'd loved her the most. And here she was with a man she loved but who didn't love her. For the first time in a long while she felt the weight of her loneliness.

Brooke tasted her tears before she felt them streaming down her face. She sensed his presence before she saw him. She wiped her cheeks and turned away, but Jameson knelt in front of her and cupped her chin, forcing her to look at him.

"Never be ashamed of feeling sad," he said in a quiet voice. "If the dog really bothers you, I'll tell Cecelia to keep him inside."

"No, it's not that," she sniffed. "It's just memories."

"I know losing your father must still hurt."

"I'm just feeling sorry for myself because I'm also a little angry at him. I have so many unanswered questions. I'm still angry that he put that stipulation in his will and forced me to get married just so I could keep what rightfully belongs to me."

Jameson pulled her into his arms and held her. And just as his show of kindness had increased her sorrow in the past, it did the same now. She didn't want him to just comfort her; she didn't want understanding words and compassion. She wanted his heart. She wanted him to ask her to be more than his lover. She cried even harder because Meredith had had him first and had been his first love, and he probably still loved her. She wanted to tear down the wall Jameson had built around his heart and force him to trust her. She wanted to tell him that she'd never break his heart and she would love him until the day she died.

But she knew that would not happen so, as she had done so many times before, she pushed down her sadness and settled for recognizing futility. If she was going to survive this year with him, she had to be realistic. She had to realize that no matter what she did, he wouldn't see her as anything more than Meredith's little sister. Not as a woman in her own right. She drew away from him. "I'm much better now," she said, putting on a smile even though she felt hollow inside.

"Are you sure?"

She stood. "Positive."

Jameson brooded as he walked the estate that evening. Brooke didn't want to be there. She could pretend that she was just missing her father, but he sensed more than that. He knew she was missing her home, her old life. She didn't want to be a rancher's wife. Damn Ray Palmer for forcing her into a marriage she clearly didn't want. He hated seeing Brooke unhappy, but he didn't know what to do to fix whatever was the matter. He could buy her anything, but she'd made it clear that she didn't want anything from him.

As he was beginning to have more feelings for her, he believed that she was just feeling more trapped. He'd wanted to comfort her more, but he'd felt her need to withdraw from him. He remembered walking the estate eleven years earlier after Meredith had left him. What was wrong with him? Why did he keep falling for women who wanted a different life than he did? At least he didn't love Brooke, and that was his saving grace. He liked her a lot, but he hadn't made himself as vulnerable as he had when he was twenty-two. He wouldn't, couldn't plan and think about a future with Brooke because he knew there wouldn't be one.

Early one afternoon, Brooke went into the stables to check on Royal Thunder. Jameson had been more quiet the past few days and being with the horse reminded her of when things between she and Jameson had been more carefree. She stopped when she saw Laney on the other side of the horse stroking him. She took a step back, ready to leave, when Laney turned then lifted her hand and waved. Brooke found the gesture surprising; Laney had appeared cold over the past several weeks.

"I'm just checking in on the patient," Laney said, once Brooke was close.

"He's doing well."

"He's not the only one you've healed." Laney tilted her head. "I've never seen Jameson so happy. I'm really glad you married him."

"Really?"

"Yes." She smiled. "You sound surprised."

I am. "It's just…I thought you didn't like me. I understand, especially after what my sister did."

Laney's smile faded and a tint of sadness entered her gaze. "I'm sorry I gave you that impression. I've just had a lot on my mind. It has nothing to do with you."

"Your mother said you're melancholy because you're feeling the letdown from being out of the Olympic spotlight."

Laney laughed bitterly. "As if."

"If it's not that, then what is it?"

Laney shook her head.

"We're sisters now, remember?" Brooke said, sensing Laney had something she wanted to share. "You helped me, so let me help you."

"You can't help me."

"Why not?"

Laney bit her lip. "I'm pregnant." She let her voice drop. "Almost four months."

"Four months?" Brooke stared down at Laney's slim figure. "But you look great. I mean…" She didn't really know what to say.

Laney lightly patted her stomach. "I'm not showing yet, but that won't last long."

"You can't keep this to yourself. Your family—"

"I'm going to tell them soon but in my own time. Please don't say anything," she said, her eyes filling with tears. "I just needed someone to share this with instead of feeling so alone."

Brooke moved closer and hugged her. "I'm glad it was me. You don't need to worry about anything. I'll be there for you."

"You want us to do what?" Gwendolyn asked.

Jameson had gathered the family in the Main Room. All of the Browards were there except Brooke because she was the topic of conversation. He'd finally gotten over the scare of the car incident, convincing himself that he'd been more angry than afraid, and now that they were on safer ground he wanted to do something extra special for her. Although Brooke had enough pieces for the upcoming auction, she was disappointed that she hadn't been able to get any of the shale. What she had managed to get out of the cave had been lost when the car had plunged into the ravine. And she had envisioned creating several unique pieces of pottery using the shale. Yesterday Jameson had found her searching frantically in her studio.

"What's wrong?" He had come up behind her and held her.

"I don't have anything to work with."

He looked around the studio, confused. She had plenty of material. "Yes, you do."

She threw up her hands. "I have ordinary clay, but I had wanted to create something special. Something spectacular."

"You don't need anything special. What you already have will do. You're the artist. What you make is already spectacular."

"But…"

"I showed Linda pictures of your work. She was ecstatic that you're willing to donate some of your pottery for the auction. Besides, there will be other items up for sale by other local artists. You'll be the 'big name' artist and blow them all way." Brooke had smiled at him but he could see she hadn't been fully convinced so he wanted to do something to help her gain confidence.

"I want you all to bid on her work," Jameson repeated to his family. "There's a charity auction for River Dance, the horse rescue organization and—"

"Yes, I've seen their advertising everywhere," Grandpa Charles said. "They have our name splashed all over the event. Something about Brooke's pottery."

"Yes, the event planner and president of the organization, Linda Bearclaw, and I agreed that the Broward name would help gain more interest."

"I'd have thought the word *auction* would have had you running for the hills," Wes teased, reminding his brother of the annual bachelor auction that Jameson hated.

"This is different," Jameson said. "Brooke's pottery is going to be displayed and I get to stay in the background."

"And you want us to bid on them?" Steven asked slowly, wanting to clarify his son's request. "Is her work so bad that you don't think anyone else will?"

Jameson shook his head. "No, it's not bad at all. I just want you all to help us start the bidding at the right price."

"What do you know about this charity?" Gwendolyn asked. "It's not like you to lend your name to any group with their hand out asking for money. Heaven knows, we get many requests to support this-and-that and others, but—"

"I've worked as a volunteer with this rescue for years," Jameson said, finally ready to be honest about where he'd spent his extra time. "And it's important to me."

"Ah, that explains why you ended up with that sick horse," she said. "What's his name?"

"Royal Thunder."

"Yes. That's right. Brooke told me some silly story about you getting him from a circus, but this makes more sense."

Jameson looked around the room with expectancy. "So, can I count on you?"

"Won't it look a little self-serving?" Laney asked. "I mean, Brooke is family now."

"True, but people follow our lead. If you show interest then others will, too. I just want to get it rolling."

"Okay, we're in," Steven said, speaking for the group. "I'll be the first to bid."

The day of the fund-raiser was overcast, but that didn't stop the crowds from coming. It ended up being one of the largest showings in the organization's history. The event was held in a large converted barn just outside of Granger. The items up for sale were all on display and a small brochure was distributed that included a picture of each item, the name of the artist and a brief background on what the item was made of. There was a vast array of high-end crafts including hand-woven baskets, Native American jewelry, handcrafted wall hangings and rugs, and Brooke's pottery.

"I can't believe it," Linda said. "The amount of people here is incredible."

"I'm not surprised," Jameson said.

Linda grinned and nudged him with her elbow. "Of course. You Browards are used to drawing a crowd."

"Isn't this what you wanted?"

"Much more." Linda glanced around, then frowned. "Where's the star attraction?"

"Giving more instructions to the auctioneer, no doubt."

"I don't know what she's so nervous about. She's very good."

"Hopefully she'll find that out today. And I hope soon."

Linda folded her arms and narrowed her eyes. "You're up to something."

"No, I'm not." He turned, saw Brooke ahead and waved.

Brooke waved back and joined them. "Everything is wonderful," she said, looking every part the successful artist in a two-piece white cotton outfit. She wore her hair down, allowing soft curls to frame her face.

"Thank you so much for being a part of this event," Linda said, giving Brooke a big hug.

"You're welcome."

"Everything all set?" Jameson asked her.

"I think so," Brooke said, rubbing her hands together in anticipation. "I just had to make sure the pieces traveled well. I had this nightmare that I opened the box and all the pieces were smashed. But they all look good. Then I had this horrible thought of someone carrying one of them to the stage and then tripping and dropping it and—"

"None of that is going to happen," Jameson said, resting a reassuring arm around her shoulders.

"You're going to be a hit," Linda said.

Brooke was about to reply when people started to turn to something in the doorway. Samara Lionne entered the barn.

"What is she doing here?" Brooke asked.

Jameson frowned. "I have no idea."

"Maybe she wants to grab some of the attention," Linda said.

"That doesn't make sense. This is a small-fry event for her," Jameson said.

"It's an event connected with the Browards, so it's not small," Linda said. "We wouldn't even have a reporter cover this event if you hadn't shown up. We have been holding this event for the past three years, and it's the first time we are getting so much coverage."

"True," he said. Although Jameson had been a volunteer with the group, he had never considered being involved with the auction before. "What possible reason could she have to be here?"

"Connections." Linda grinned and rested her hands on her hips. "Well, this day is going to be one to remember."

The bidding started with a frenzy. And when one of Brooke's pottery came up, Steven did his duty and started the bid with a generous offer. Soon others joined in.

"Two thousand," Samara said in a clear, loud voice.

For a moment the room went silent.

"What is she up to?" Jameson said in a harsh whisper.

"Who cares?" Linda said. "At least she's making both Brooke and the charity look good."

But Steven had the same apprehension Jameson did and lifted his card. "Twenty-two hundred."

"Twenty-five hundred."

"Twenty-eight hundred," he countered.

"What's your father doing?" Brooke asked in an anxious whisper.

"I don't know," Jameson said, but part of him did. His father saw Samara as a threat, and it wasn't just her buying Wes's land that bothered him. But Jameson didn't want his father's distrust or distaste for her to show so publicly. He raced over to his father, and by the time he did, the price of the piece had reached three thousand. "Dad, that's enough."

"Don't tell me what to do."

"Let her have it."

Steven ignored him and said, "Thirty-five hundred."

"Four thousand," Samara said.

Steven shot her a look, then glanced at Jameson and Gwen, who'd given him a look that meant it was time to step down. He could outbid any number the actress threw at him, but he knew that wasn't the point of the auction. He held his card in his lap, admitting defeat.

"Four thousand it is," the auctioneer said. "Going once, going twice and sold to the lovely lady, number seventy-four."

Steven turned and left as the next item to be auctioned became available. Jameson followed him outside. "What just happened?"

"You asked me to bid, so I did."

"I asked you to bid once."

"I wanted to make it look good," Steven said, shoving his hands in his pockets.

"Don't lie to me. I know what this is about."

Steven looked at him. "Do you?"

"You think I don't feel it, too? We know most of those people in there, and to have an outsider come in and wave their money about is much like what's happening to our town. But this is just an auction, and the money will go to good use."

"That's not the point." Steven tapped his chest. "It felt personal this time."

"You're playing with pocket change," Jameson said, knowing they could easily have paid ten thousand without blinking. "What made it feel so personal?"

"It's not about the money. It's about keeping what's ours. I don't know what came over me. I should have just let her have it, but I keep thinking about her owning the land Wes sold to her and—"

"I know," Jameson said, patting his father on the back. "But we can't be suspicious of every action she makes. Maybe she's into art or always had a fondness for horses…"

"Right, and I'm the king of Mozambique."

"I saw her press conference and I think things are going to be okay, Dad."

Steven sighed, not wanting to argue with him and hoping that the sinking feeling of unease about Samara would go away. "You're right. I made too big a deal of it."

"Come on, let's go back in. There are plenty of other items you can spend your money on."

* * *

Once the auction was over, Gwendolyn walked over to Jameson. "You've been keeping secrets."

He froze and glanced around, hoping no one could overhear them. Linda had spirited Brooke off to talk to some of the people who'd bid on her work. "What do you mean?" he asked, careful to keep his voice neutral so he wouldn't give anything away.

"Is there anything else you're not telling me?"

"I don't know what you're talking about."

"Why didn't you let us know that Brooke was this good?"

Jameson felt himself relax, glad that his other secret was safe. "She didn't feel comfortable yet and I didn't want to push her."

Gwendolyn shook her head. "Why do I have the feeling that that's not the whole story?"

"Because you have a suspicious mind? You and Dad are well matched."

"I know. Your father and I were worried about you, but we're not anymore."

"That's a relief."

"But something else has me worried."

"What?"

"Your sister. Have you had a chance to talk to her?"

"About what?" Jameson asked, knowing he couldn't tell his mother that his sister's request for a private investigator had worried him, too.

"Find out what's on her mind."

"I will, when I get a chance," he said, but he knew

that wouldn't make much of a difference because he didn't know how to make his sister open up to him.

"Or you could ask Brooke to," Gwendolyn said, seeming to sense his hesitation. "Sometimes there are things a woman feels more comfortable sharing with someone around her own age."

"I'm sure Laney is fine. She's probably still adjusting to coming back home."

"I have told myself that, too."

"What else has you worried?" Jameson asked, eager to change the subject.

"Your father. I don't know what got into him today."

"I spoke to him. He's fine now. He just got caught up in the frenzy."

"I hope you're right about that."

Jameson gave his mother's arm a light squeeze and flashed a teasing grin. "Hey, I'm the one who's supposed to be serious, not you. You're here to enjoy yourself."

She smiled. "I remember when I used to have to tell you that."

"You don't anymore."

Gwendolyn gave him a brief hug. "I'm glad."

Brooke was still in shock that Samara had bought her work. Samara Lionne, the Hollywood actress, had bought her work. Bid on it. For four thousand dollars! She felt as if it was a dream. She watched Samara go up to the podium to retrieve the piece of pottery. She had to admit, the woman had taste. That particular piece was one of Brooke's prized possessions. It had won several awards in various art shows, but she hadn't been willing to part with it before. Putting it in the auction had been a difficult choice at first, but knowing that she was helping a charity, and Jameson, made the decision easier.

"This is going to put you on the map," Linda said, as if reading her thoughts.

Brooke laughed, thinking of her ex-broker. "Matthew, my former broker, would have wept if he were here. He would never have allowed me to put it in an auction. He wouldn't be able to get his commission! I wonder why she only bid on that one piece? I doubt Western-style pottery will fit her decor."

"Who cares? Money is green and you can now advertise your work as something that women of fashion, like Samara Lionne, can have. Thank you so much for doing this."

For the first time, Brooke felt like a real artist. She was. Her work wasn't about her having a pretty face; it stood on its own merit. Although she suspected that Jameson had probably persuaded his father to place a high bid, it was the other offers that had caught her attention. Her work was good and now she knew the direction she wanted to go.

Brooke turned to Linda. "I don't want this partnership to end. I would like to come up with a special line of pottery and have part of the proceeds go to the River Dance rescue."

"That would be wonderful." Linda hugged Brooke again, this time nearly smothering her with her long hair. "I had a professional photographer take pictures of all the items in the auction prior to the bidding. I'll make sure to send them to you so that you can post them on your website and go from there." Linda turned and called out to someone in the crowd. "I need to go. I've got to talk to that man." She ran off.

Gwendolyn then approached Brooke. "My dear, your work is beautiful. I had no idea you were this good. Do you take commissions?"

"I never thought to. I usually just create what's in my heart."

"Well, if you're ever interested, let me know. Also, I know that people who visit the lodge enjoy souvenirs. We could create a side business featuring your work. Would you be interested?"

"I'd love it."

Everything felt right. Unlike her wedding day, Brooke didn't feel alone. She had come to know the Browards as a caring, loyal and loving family. When she saw Jameson she hurried over to him. "What did you say to your father? Do you want me to thank him?"

"For what?"

"He started the bidding so high on my work." Brooke started to smile. "I know you asked him to."

"It would have started high anyway. You underestimate how good you really are. That Rainey guy never let you know how much he was making off you and didn't want you to know how good you were. As for my dad, I just gave him a nudge in the right direction. He sort of got carried away. But this was a good distraction for him and my family. He's got a lot on his mind."

"The land buying?"

Jameson looked surprised.

"I know you rarely talk about it, but I know it's on your family's mind. It's on the mind of most of the people in Granger."

"His more than most."

"Don't worry so much. I'm sure things will work out."

"I saw you talking to my mother. Was she trying to persuade you to talk to Laney?"

Brooke stiffened. "Why would she want me to do that?"

"Because she's a mother and she's concerned. I don't want to bother you, but if you could talk to my sister, it might help."

Brooke plastered on a smile. "Sure," she said, pained that she couldn't tell either Jameson or Gwendolyn what Laney's troubles really were. They would both find out soon enough.

That evening, Brooke thought about the auction and Laney's confession as she sat in the Shank of the Evening saloon. She didn't know how the Browards would take the news. Laney had sounded so alone and scared. Brooke knew the feeling. She wished she could confess her love for Jameson, and she knew how painful and lonely it had been to be his fake wife when she desperately wanted it to be real. When the year was through, she'd be all alone again. She was lost in thought when a large cowboy hat dropped onto the table. She glanced up and saw Mitch. "You still offering to cook my hat?"

"Any way you like it."

He took a seat. "You really pulled it off. You've got

everyone fooled, even the Browards. Everything happened just the way your father wanted."

Brooke frowned. "What are you talking about?"

Mitch swore. "I knew I had one beer too many. Forget it. I've said too much already."

"And you're going to say a lot more. I know you're
not drunk, so don't lie to me."

Mitch glanced around. "Let's not talk about it here."

"Explain what you mean," Brooke said in a tight
voice.

Mitch released a heavy sigh. "The will. Your father
didn't just want you to get married. He wanted to make
sure you got married to Jameson."

Chapter 17

Jameson was polishing his horse saddle when he caught a glimpse of his father coming up the driveway. He inwardly groaned, wondering if it was going to be a casual chat or another subtle dig at his marriage. He set the saddle aside and went to meet him.

"Hi," he said. "You have some news?"

"No," Steven said, stepping out of his car. "I just want to talk."

That did not sound like a good sign. "Okay, let's go inside."

"I'd rather walk, if you don't mind."

"Fine." They walked several yards in silence, and when it appeared his father wasn't going to introduce a topic, Jameson did. "I saw Samara Lionne's press conference. She handles herself well. Perhaps we don't have to worry too much about her."

"I want to believe that, too."

"But you don't?"

"No. I've lived long enough to always question people's true motives."

"Is that why you're here?" Jameson asked, ready to take on another round of his father's suspicions."

"Yes, I owe you an apology," Steven said.

Jameson stopped walking. "For what?"

Steven continued walking and didn't look back. "For ever doubting you about Brooke."

Jameson stared at his father's back, trying to comprehend his unexpected confession. He hurried to catch up with him. "I don't understand."

"I'm admitting that I was wrong. I haven't seen you this happy in years."

"But I haven't done anything different."

"Not according to Frank."

"What? Is he spying on me?"

"No, he's happy for you. He said the mood around the ranch has improved because of you. That you've gotten a new cow dog to help with the work. That you're like your old self when you took ranching as a calling instead of a sentence." Steven patted Jameson on the shoulder. "It's nice to have the man I remember. Your mother was right—married life suits you."

Brooke sat in Mitch's truck, staring sightlessly ahead, trying to understand all he'd told her. She'd had a wild desire to cover his mouth to stop him from talking. To pretend that they'd never spoken so she could stay ignorant of the truth. It would have been easier that way. It would have saved her pride. But now her pride was in tatters. "He did it for a dream?" Brooke repeated.

Mitch nodded, looking miserable. "He had long envisioned the Palmer and Broward families being bonded and creating a larger empire. You know, similar to what Steven Broward had done with his marriage to Gwendolyn Webb. Meredith ruined his plans by leaving Jameson and running off to New York. So I agreed to help make his wish come true by suggesting you marry Jameson. I had a hunch you were sweet on him anyway, and it didn't take much nudging for you to take up the idea on your own."

"But in the bar you said you thought our marriage was fake and—"

"It was all an act."

"Why would you do such a thing? If I hadn't married, you would have gotten the ranch outright."

Mitch shook his head. "Ray was my best friend and more of a father to me than my own father ever was. Ray made his request on his deathbed. I made a promise that went beyond personal gain."

"A promise? You allowed my father to treat us like chess pieces because of a promise? You allowed him to manipulate and connive us?"

"It wasn't like that."

"Well, you should feel great," Brooke said in a bitter tone. "You've done your duty and succeeded, so you don't have to feel guilty. You're now released from that promise. And I'm going to free all of us from my father's greed. I'm going to ask Jameson for a divorce and then you can have the ranch fair and square." For the first time in weeks, Brooke began to doubt herself. Did she really know her own mind, or was she acting like a puppet based on something that had been fabricated by her father and Mitch just to get her to marry Jameson?

She remembered how in his later years her father kept talking about how Jameson Broward would have made a great son-in-law if Meredith had played her cards right. She hadn't taken any notice of what he was saying but had found it odd that he would phone and ask Jameson for advice whenever he could. But Brooke hadn't thought that there was a motive behind what he was doing. Besides, she always liked seeing Jameson, even if it was usually from a distance.

But now she felt totally confused. Her father had manipulated her and her childhood crush and for selfish reasons. He'd used her emotions as a weapon against her. Did she really love Jameson, or had that been planted in her mind, too?

"No, Brooke. Don't think about a divorce. You don't want to do that."

"Are you still trying to tell me my own mind?"

"I know it's a shock, but—"

"Shut up. I'm getting a divorce and you're not stopping me." She jumped out of the truck and slammed the door.

He'd used her. Her own father had used her. All the time she had been at home, playing the dutiful daughter, he had been crafting a plan to force her to marry Jameson. She remembered the last time they had been together. Her father had asked her if she had any friends. She had found that odd; she had a decent social life. Then he'd told her not to stay away from the Browards because of the mistake Meredith made. She had found that request strange, but once again, she hadn't thought much about it. But now she questioned every action he'd made. Had any of it been genuine? She'd thought he'd wanted her to get married so she wouldn't be lonely, but he hadn't cared about that. Had he ever cared about her happiness? About anyone's happiness except his own?

It didn't matter now. She was free of him. She wouldn't let him toy with her life anymore. She would tell Jameson goodbye. She steeled herself for the task she had to do. She would make it quick and painless. Besides, he'd feel relieved.

Brooke found him in the stables tending to one of the horses. He held a hoof between his thighs. As he heard her enter, he turned to her and smiled. It melted her heart. "Come here," he said.

Wordlessly, she moved toward him.

Jameson took off his hat and put it on her head. "You've earned it."

Brooke blinked back tears as he led the horse back to its stall. She didn't want to say goodbye. Not yet.

"Did you want to tell me something?" Jameson asked.

Brooke threw her arms around him and kissed him. "Take me. Right here. Right now," she whispered against his lips. "And don't ask me if I'm sure."

"There are some young horses here."

"We won't be doing anything they haven't seen before. Besides, they won't spot us in the hayloft." She slid her hand down his chest. "And you're already half-dressed." She scrambled up the ladder then looked down at him. "Don't be shy."

"I told you I'm not shy."

"Then what's taking you so long?" she asked, taking off her shoes.

Jameson climbed up and stared at her. "I'm just not used to seeing you like this."

Brooke unbuttoned her blouse. "You've forgotten how I look naked?"

"No, but—"

"Stop talking," Brooke said, tossing her blouse to the side. She unlatched her bra. "We can do that later."

But no matter how much she taunted him, Jameson didn't move toward her. His dark gaze was heated but unreadable. She didn't want him to suspect anything, so she flashed a naughty grin then rested her foot against the hard bulge in his jeans. "Oh, good, you are ready. I was starting to get worried."

He grabbed her foot. "You never have to worry about me being ready for you." He knelt beside her and helped her out of her jeans. "I could never get enough of this," he said, his hand sliding down her stomach to the swell of her hips.

She undid his jeans. "Me either."

Soon his body was on top of hers and she reveled in the warmth of his soft flesh. She arched into him, welcoming him deeper inside her.

Brooke used her body to tell him the story of her heart. She told him how much she loved him. How happy he made her. How she wished they could start a family together and that she had never wanted to leave him. She made her body say what she couldn't because at the moment she wasn't sure if what she had called love had really been that or had just the feelings of a young woman who had been manipulated into thinking she was really in love.

Jameson lay on his back and laughed. "How come every time I give you something, we end up making love like there's no tomorrow?"

Because there won't be a tomorrow for us this time, Brooke thought. But she didn't say anything; she kissed him again, knowing it would be the last time.

Brooke couldn't pack her bags fast enough. If she took a moment to think about what she was doing she would stop. She'd find excuses to stay. She would convince herself that deceiving him for a few more months would be okay. Because she did know her own mind and she did love him. But she'd discovered the truth, and Jameson deserved to hear it. She'd thought about leaving him a note, but that wouldn't be fair. She'd put all her things in her car first and then tell him.

"What are you doing?"

She spun around and looked at Jameson's stunned face, her heart pounding. "I'm leaving."

"Why?"

Jameson came into the room and closed the door. "Aren't you the same woman I was just with in the hayloft yesterday?"

She briefly closed her eyes. "Yes, but—"

"I thought we both had a good time. Was I wrong?"

Brooke turned away from him and put another stack of shirts into her suitcase. "Please don't make this harder than it has to be."

Jameson crossed the room and closed the suitcase. "What has to be hard? I don't understand. Why are you leaving?"

"Because I have to. I want a divorce."

"I still don't understand why you want this," Jameson said with anger. He took a deep breath and softened his tone. "I know you've been unhappy. I know it's been hard for you being here with me, but I'm doing my best. Just tell me what I have done. Tell me what you want me to do."

"You haven't done anything." She sat down on the bed as if she had no more energy to stand. "We were both manipulated from the start. I won't hold you in a marriage you never wanted. I spoke to Mitch and he told me that my father used us as pawns in his own game. He wanted to tie our families together in any way he could. Since you didn't end up marrying Meredith, he thought I'd be a good replacement. I can't stay another day here knowing that we've both been played for fools."

She wanted a divorce. Jameson stared at Brooke, speechless. He'd been prepared for a lot of things, but he hadn't been prepared for this. He now couldn't imagine his life without her. In just weeks she'd become the most important person in his life.

"Look, let's just think this through. You don't have to leave yet."

"Yes, I do." She jumped to her feet. "I'll come back for my other things later." She pushed past him and headed for the door.

He seized her wrist. "Wait."

Brooke stopped but didn't turn to him. "What?"

"Let's talk about this."

"There's nothing more to say." She slowly spun around and faced him. "I've thought it through. Don't try to be brave and pretend that you're not just as angry as I am. I know you're a man of honor, and that's why I'm making this decision for both of us. I don't care if everyone finds out what our marriage really was about. If you want to come up with your own story for our breakup, I'll go along with it, but I won't live this lie another day."

Jameson didn't release his hold on her wrist, desperate to find the right words to stop her from leaving. He'd told himself he wouldn't ask her to stay. That he'd never face the risk of rejection again. But now that vow felt meaningless, just as his life would feel without Brooke. "I want you to stay."

"Why?"

Jameson took a deep breath. He had to say what he'd been to afraid to say after her car accident. Words that had burned in his heart for weeks. "Because I love you," he said, his voice raw with emotion. His love hadn't been enough before and he feared it wouldn't be so again. "When I saved you from your car and held you, I didn't want to let go. I knew that you belonged in my life and I couldn't imagine it without you." He shook his head. "I know you only married me to save your inheritance, but if you give me a chance, in time I think you'll grow to love me, too."

Brooke stared at Jameson, unsure whether she should laugh or cry. "I've loved you since I was fifteen, when you first started dating my sister. When I faced death all I could think about was being separated from you and I wanted to tell you how I felt, but I never dreamed you could feel the same way about me. Being married to you was what I have been dreaming about all my life."

"Well, your dream has come true." He pulled her close to him. "For a special wedding gift, and with your permission, I plan to buy out Meredith's half of the Palmer ranch. And I want to give you a real honeymoon. Where do you want to go?"

"But we can't leave now. There's too much going on with Granger."

"The BWB Ranch can survive a few weeks without me. I no longer have a mistress. I only have place in my heart for one true love and that's you. And I promise to spend the rest of my life proving that to you."

* * * * *

REQUEST YOUR FREE BOOKS!

2 FREE NOVELS
PLUS 2 FREE GIFTS!

KIMANI™
ROMANCE

Love's ultimate destination!